Readers love the
...cker Springs series

...rves End

"Warm and fuzzies, right here! I really enjoyed this!"
—*Divine Magazine*

"*Where Nerves End* was a breathtakingly beautiful story, full of angst, passion and coming out… I loved this story."

—TTC Books and More

Second Hand

"I loved this book and am so glad I got to spend time with El and Paul."

—Diverse Reader

"This was an enjoyable read with a very satisfying happily ever after. I loved seeing Paul come into his own and choose El above all others."

—Open Skye Book Reviews

"I can always count on Marie Sexton and Heidi Cullinan... If you're in the mood for something sexy and
...   d a great

...   ok Banter

By MARIE SEXTON

With Heidi Cullinan: Family Man
Lost Along the Way
Tales of the Curious Cookbook

CODA
Promises • Putting out Fires
A to Z • The Letter Z • Paris A to Z
Strawberries for Dessert
Fear, Hope, and Bread Pudding
Shotgun
The Letter Z & Paris A to Z Anthology

TUCKER SPRINGS
By L.A. Witt: Where Nerves End
With Heidi Cullinan: Second Hand
By Heidi Cullinan: Dirty Laundry
By L.A. Witt: Covet Thy Neighbor
Never a Hero

WRENCH WARS
By L.A. Witt: Last Mechanic Standing
Normal Enough
By L.A. Witt: Wrenches, Regrets, and Reality Checks
Making Waves
With L.A. Witt: Wrench Wars Anthology

Published by DREAMSPINNER PRESS
www.dreamspinnerpress.com

NEVER A HERO

MARIE SEXTON

Published by
DREAMSPINNER PRESS

5032 Capital Circle SW, Suite 2, PMB# 279,
Tallahassee, FL 32305-7886 USA
www.dreamspinnerpress.com

Mass Market Paperback ISBN: 978-1-64108-129-0
Trade Paperback ISBN: 978-1-64080-908-6
Digital ISBN: 978-1-64080-907-9
Library of Congress Control Number: 2019930012
Mass Market Paperback published 2019
v. 1.0
Second Edition
First Edition published by Riptide Publishing, May 2013.

Printed in the United States of America
∞
This paper meets the requirements of
ANSI/NISO Z39.48-1992 (Permanence of Paper).

To Zoe, who inspired this book, even though she's way too young to be allowed to read it.

And most importantly, to her mother, Kristin, who's amazing in every way and gives me fabulous material all the time whether she knows it or not. Love you to pieces!

Acknowledgments

WITH MANY thanks to Rowan, who is always a tremendous help.

Also, thank you to Lori and Heidi for bearing with me.

Chapter One

IT TOOK three years for me to convince myself I was in love with my downstairs neighbor. It only took one day for her to move out of my life.

It wasn't her fault. It wasn't as if I'd ever told her how I felt. In truth, I'd barely spoken to her, outside of the general pleasantries between neighbors when we passed on the walk or ran into each other in our shared backyard. But I'd watched her. Not in a stalker kind of way. But some days, when she was out in the garden, I'd sit on my porch and read so I could catch glimpses of her through the flowers as she knelt in the dirt, her fingers sunk into the cold Colorado soil.

But what had really made me love her was listening to her.

Her name was Regina, and she was a pianist. Not a concert pianist, or even an aspiring one. She had a day job somewhere in town, doing what, I didn't know, but for three years, I'd seen her leave at seven forty-five and come home at five twenty. For an hour or so, she'd be out of my sight, in her own apartment below mine. But sometime around six thirty or seven, she'd always start to play, and I'd lie on the couch in my living room, directly above her piano, and think about how I could learn to love a woman like her.

But now here she was, moving out.

I watched out my window as she loaded boxes into a truck. She had help. Two men and one woman. I barely noticed the woman, but I studied the men. One was smaller, studious-looking, glasses perched on his nose. A bit twitchy about touching the boxes or going into the house. I dubbed him The Academic. The other was bigger. Huge, in fact. Clearly one of those men who spent hours in the gym. He lugged boxes out to the truck two and three at a time.

The Hero.

Not that he was Regina's hero, though. The men were obviously a couple, although I tried not to notice how happy they looked together. The lingering glances and the secret smiles. For three years I'd lived only a few blocks from the Light District in Tucker Springs, and for three years I'd told myself it wasn't the place for me. All I needed was to meet the right woman, and maybe all those other thoughts that snuck into my head late at night would disappear. Regina could help me erase the embarrassed regret of my high school years and the loneliness that had haunted me since college. If Regina and I were a couple, I'd told myself, her playing would get me through the tough times. Whenever I started wondering how it felt to be on my knees in front of another man, whenever I started thinking about what I really wanted, I could turn to her and say, "Play something for me." And she'd smile at me, pleased that I wanted to hear her latest piece, and as her fingers would dance over the keys, teasing Bach or Beethoven or Mozart from that big square box, I'd fall in love with her again and forget about the fact that it was men who turned my head, time and again.

Except now she was moving.

I pulled the shade down and turned away. I didn't want to watch her leave.

I also didn't want to watch two men who could openly admit they were in love.

"Owen, you're an idiot," I told myself. After all, a braver man would have offered to help. A more confident man would have taken this last opportunity to talk to her. Maybe get her phone number. A forwarding address in case there was mail or a package. In case she wanted to have dinner some night. A whole man would have offered to help her move. An undamaged man wouldn't have been afraid to walk out and say, "Hey, let me lend you a hand."

I laughed suddenly at my own thoughts. How ironic that I'd think of one of my least-favorite phrases in the English language. I didn't exactly have a hand to spare.

I looked down at my left arm, where it ended in a smooth tapered stump just below my elbow.

"Let me lend you a hand," I said out loud. "But it's the only one I have, so I'll need it back when you're done."

It wasn't as absurd as it sounded. I could have helped. It wasn't like I couldn't carry a damn box. Not two or three at a time, like The Hero, but that didn't make me worthless.

No, it wasn't my missing arm that stopped me from helping Regina move. It was the way they'd all react, sorting carefully through the boxes, deciding which ones I could carry. Nothing too heavy. Nothing breakable. Certainly not the glassware or the boxes of books. Linens, though. Linens they might let me carry.

Or pillows. Even a one-armed man could carry pillows.

I'd never be anybody's hero.

"Stop feeling sorry for yourself," I muttered.

I was startled by a knock on the door. I was even more surprised to open it and find Regina on the other side. I stood as I always did, with the left half of my body hidden behind the door. Certainly she knew by now about my missing arm, but I'd learned people didn't like to see it.

"Hi, Erwin!" she said. It was an indicator of how little we'd actually talked. She didn't even know my name.

I was slow to answer, making sure my tongue was ready to move. I'd beaten my stutter years ago, but it still appeared sometimes, usually at the least-opportune moments. "Ready to go?" I asked her, gesturing toward the truck.

"Yep, this is it!" She held a set of keys out for me. "I told the landlord I'd leave the spares with you."

I held out my right hand and let the keys fall into my palm. I thought about the one thing I hadn't seen The Hero carry out her door. "What about your piano?"

She shrugged and ran a hand through her short hair. There was more gray in it than I'd realized. When I'd imagined a life with her, I'd made her my age, but I was reminded now of the fact that she was actually more than ten years my senior, although she looked damn good for her age. "I'm leaving it. It wasn't mine to begin with. It belonged to whoever lived here before me, and anyway, it'd be a pain in the ass to move."

"Will you buy a new one?"

"I don't know. Maybe eventually. But mostly it takes up space and gathers dust, you know?"

She'd played almost every night. Certainly she loved it. I'd made myself believe she loved it. How else could I possibly love her?

"Anyway," she said, suddenly awkward. "Take care."

Take care.

Then she turned around and walked away. Down the sidewalk to the truck. Away from the imaginary life she'd unknowingly starred in.

Away from me.

TWO DAYS later the scene was repeated in reverse. A Tahoe and a pickup filled with furniture and boxes parked in front of the house. A total of four men got out and walked through the bright autumn leaves littering the lawn to the side of the house, out of my line of sight.

I should introduce myself. Find out who exactly was moving in and give him the spare key.

That's what I told myself, but I knew I wouldn't do it. Not until I was forced to.

I heard laughter downstairs, then piano notes. Not a real song like Regina had played. Not the practiced music of a pianist, but the inexpert jangle of random tones as somebody tested the instrument. I pictured one of the men leaning against Regina's piano, hitting the keys, laughing with his friends at his own lack of skill.

"Don't quit your day job!" one of them said.

The house I lived in had been built as a split-level in the seventies, but had been broken up into two separate apartments. Mine consisted of what had once been the main floor, which meant my door opened onto the front porch. The lower apartment was reached via a stairway at the side of the house. The setup was unusual in that the house was built on a hill and had a walk-out basement, making the downstairs living space far more tolerable than most basement apartments. I listened to the men below as they wandered through the apartment, looking in closets and kitchen cabinets, opening the sliding glass door to look at our shared backyard. Most times, their words were indistinguishable, but their laughter carried clearly through the vents. It had been a long time since I'd shared that kind of easy laughter with anybody.

For the first time, I regretted having an apartment below me.

Luckily the torture didn't last long. Soon enough, the laughter stopped and the moving began. I watched for a few minutes through my window. Like before, two of the men were clearly a couple. They were happy and stupidly in love, one of them tall and thin and dark, the other shorter and strawberry blond. I immediately hated them for their easy, open affection. I hoped they weren't the ones moving in.

I turned my attention to the other two. Neither was as big as The Hero, although one of them in particular was obviously well acquainted with the gym. His arms bulged under the short sleeves of his shirt. Dark blond hair and laughing eyes. I couldn't decide if he and the fourth man, whose arms were covered with tattoos, were lovers or not. Friends certainly, but if they were more, they at least didn't glow with the bright, electric giddiness of the other two.

Four able-bodied men. Not a missing limb among them.

I didn't even think about offering to help.

Instead, I went to my computer and worked. After all, I had bills to pay. My mother had insisted that I learn to type one-handed, using home row as my base, keeping my index finger on the F and my pinky on the J. She'd demanded I master the ability, insisting it was a skill I'd need. I resented my mother for a lot of things, but in this, I was glad I'd done as instructed. I could type one-handed as well as many people could with two, and missing my left hand didn't diminish my ability to use a mouse. I put on my headphones and lost the afternoon to work, designing newsletters and brochures for a local marketing company. I didn't necessarily love my job, but I was good at it, and it allowed me the luxury of working from home. My music drowned out the sound of the men bumping down the outside steps with boxes and furniture.

It wasn't until long after I'd quit working for the day that the knock came—not from the front door where one might expect it, but from the sliding glass door in the dining room, which meant whoever was knocking must have come through the shared backyard and up the stairs to my elevated patio. I rounded the corner from my hallway and saw the blond with the big arms waving at me through the glass.

Too late to pretend I wasn't home.

I slid the door aside, painfully aware of the fact that I couldn't hide the left half of my body from his view. "Yes?"

"Hey!" he said, holding his right hand out to me. "I'm Nick Reynolds. I just moved in downstairs. I thought I should introduce myself since we're neighbors now."

He was cute. That was the first thought that came into my mind. Really goddamn cute, like the clichéd boy-next-door but with attitude. The smart-assed altar boy. The kid who always made wisecracks in class, yet managed to charm the teachers into not caring. The kind of guy every girl wanted to date. The kind of guy who radiated confidence.

The kind of guy I'd never be.

"Nice to meet you," he said. His hand was still out in front of him, and I realized with a start that I'd been staring stupidly at him since I'd opened the door. I reached out and let him shake my hand. He was taller than me, but not by much, with a firm grip.

"Owen Meade," I managed to say.

"Owen." His smile grew bigger. "Listen, I wondered if you'd like to come down and meet the girls. It's a mess down there 'cause I haven't had a chance to unpack anything, and there are boxes everywhere and no place to sit except the floor, but you'll have to meet them eventually, and probably sooner's better than later since we'll be sharing a backyard, don't you think?"

I suddenly wished I'd paid a bit more attention when he was moving in. Girls had moved in with him? Not just one either. Girls, plural. Either he was the luckiest SOB in town, or he was a single father. "Girls?"

"Yeah. Well, two girls, technically. One boy."

"Uh…."

"Unless you're allergic to dogs or something."

"Dogs?"

His smile disappeared and was replaced by sudden concern. "You're not, are you? Allergic, I mean? Or scared of them? 'Cause they're great dogs, really. Although Bonny will get into your trash every chance she gets, so you'll want to keep it in the garage. Do you keep it in the garage? Not on the back porch, right?" He looked around the porch, which did not in fact contain any garbage. "Good. That's good. Other than that, I promise they won't cause you a bit of trouble. And don't worry about the yard either. I'll keep it clean, so you don't have to worry about landmines or anything."

"Landmines?" It was a stupid word to latch on to, but he was talking so fast, and I wasn't used to talking to people in person. Email was more my speed.

He laughed as if I'd made a joke. "Right. So how about it?"

I blinked at him, trying to figure out what he'd asked me. Several questions, and now I wasn't sure which one to answer.

"I'm sorry," I said, feeling like a fool. "What exactly are you asking me?"

He smiled at me, and I began to blush for no good reason. To my surprise, he blushed too. "I'm talking really fast, aren't I?"

I laughed, feeling relieved it wasn't just me. "Kind of, yeah."

"I do that sometimes. Especially when I'm tired." He reached up to touch his hair, a gesture that spoke more of nervous habit than vanity. "Anyway. The real question is, do you want to come down and meet the dogs? Maybe hang out and have a beer?"

Hang out and have a beer. Such a simple concept, and yet it caused my heart to swell.

"I'd love to," I said, and I was surprised at how much I meant it.

THE DOGS were named Betty, Bert, and Bonny. Betty was a shaggy white dog, about the size of a small golden retriever. She ran in circles around my ankles. Bert was a giant, heavy-bodied yellow Lab mix. He sat stoically in front of me, his thick tail thumping against the floor. Bonny was about knee height, colored like a Doberman but built like a pony keg on Popsicle sticks.

"Humane Society guesses she's half shepherd, half beagle. Can you believe that?" Nick smiled and shook his head, looking down at her. She was the only one who wasn't interested in me. She seemed far more interested in sniffing every inch of the kitchen. "She can jump five-foot fences without missing a beat, and she's smarter than any dog has a right to be, I'll tell you that. Makes me appreciate the dumb ones a bit more, you know?" He moved a box off a kitchen chair and motioned me toward it. "Sit down."

I did, and immediately had Bert and Betty's heads in my lap. I put my right hand out and let them both sniff and nuzzle me. I stroked Bert's head, then reached for Betty. As I did, Bert nudged his head against my left arm. He didn't care there wasn't a hand there, so I rubbed his neck with the rounded end of my arm while petting Betty.

"You'll be their new best friend," Nick said.

I suddenly became aware of his eyes on me. Of the fact that I was sitting in front of him with my greatest insecurity exposed. Usually I didn't leave the house without a long sleeve covering my stump, and now here I was, not only with it uncovered, but using it as if it were a whole, useful limb. It was something that often made people uncomfortable, but when I looked up at him, he wasn't looking at my ruined arm. He also wasn't doing what most people did, straining so hard to *not* look at it that I could almost smell their discomfort. Instead, he was shaking his head at his dogs.

"Go lie down, guys!"

"They're fine."

He laughed. "You say that now, but they'll have you petting them all night." He turned and pulled a beer out of the fridge, twisted the top off, and handed me the bottle. "Here. Drink this. Please. The guys brought them for moving day but didn't finish them. Somebody should drink them."

"What about you?"

"I don't drink."

I looked down at the open beer in my hand, thinking about how Nick hadn't hesitated to open it. Every other time somebody had handed me a beer, they'd done it with the top on. I could hold the bottle against my body with my left arm and open it with my right hand, but that always led to them either apologizing and offering to do it for me or turning away and pretending they didn't notice my awkwardness. Not with Nick. There hadn't even been the telltale split second of hesitation as he wondered how to handle the situation. Maybe he would have opened it for anybody. Maybe the fact that I had only one hand had nothing to do with it.

Why did it matter so much, anyway?

I took a drink of beer while Nick went about clearing off another chair to sit in. His arms flexed as he shifted boxes. Hints of tattoo ink peeked from beneath his sleeves. When he bent over, his T-shirt rode up a bit in the back. His pants weren't low enough to make it embarrassing, but I could see the curve of his back, the way the soft flesh of his sides dipped toward his spine. I could imagine the way that bit of skin would feel under my hand.

I took a gulp of beer and looked away from him as he turned to sit down, rather than be caught staring. The kitchen was small and packed with boxes. From where I sat, I could see into what would have been the dining room, except instead of a table and chairs, it held Regina's baby grand piano. So many times I'd heard her playing it, and yet this was the first time I'd seen it. The lid was closed, and like everything else, it was covered with boxes.

"Takes up a hell of a lot of room."

"She used to play every night. I can't believe she left it."

"Huh." But he clearly wasn't interested in Regina or her piano. Instead he was staring at my left arm. "Amniotic band?" He asked the question without apology or embarrassment.

I felt a blush begin to creep up my neck. I nodded. Yes, it had been an amniotic band that had robbed me of my arm when I was still in utero. It occurred in approximately one of every twelve hundred live births. Not so terribly rare, and yet sometimes I felt as if it made me a freak, like I was the only person walking around who wasn't 100 percent complete. And yet I found Nick's candor refreshing. A lifetime of living with such a simple disability, but I'd never had anybody but doctors address me about it with such openness. "How'd you know?"

He shrugged. "Just a guess. My sister's your opposite. Missing her right arm." He touched his forearm. "About the same placement too."

I looked down at the pink tapered end of my missing arm. I put my hand over it, trying to hide it, and yet when I looked at Nick, it was obvious he wasn't thinking about my missing arm at all. He was looking around at the piles of boxes stacked ominously around us.

"God, moving sucks," he sighed. "It'll be months before I get all this shit unpacked."

"Where'd you move here from?"

"Across town." His gaze was sheepish. "Got busted by my landlord."

"Like, with drugs or something?"

He gestured at the dogs now sprawled around us on the kitchen floor. "Dogs. I only had Bert when I signed the lease, but more kept turning up, needing homes."

"What do you do?"

"I'm a veterinarian. I have an office downtown."

That surprised me, although I couldn't have said why. He was so comfortably good-looking. So casually sexy. Somehow I'd expected him to have a glamorously dangerous job. Like a race car driver, although there were no race car tracks in Tucker Springs. The idea of him as some kind of doctor, spending his days helping wounded animals, only added to his charm.

Charm I was suddenly desperate to ignore.

"So you're alone?" I asked, looking around at the boxes. "I thought maybe the guy with the tattoos…."

I let my words trail to a halt, wondering if the question was too personal, hoping I hadn't offended him by assuming he was gay, but he smiled. "Seth? No." He leaned a little closer. "I'm not seeing anyone at the moment."

My heart began to race. I'd only thought to make small talk, to get my mind off how attractive he was, and I'd managed to make things a hundred times worse. The implication of his words filled me with something that was part dread, part absolute joy. I didn't trust myself to speak without my old stutter appearing. "Oh," was all I managed to say.

He leaned closer, and I felt compelled to meet his gaze. He had dark blue eyes, and they bored into me with a directness that was unnerving. "Are you single?"

Yes! Yes, I'm single.

Fast on the tail of that thought came the fact that he had no idea how fucked-up I was.

"Uh…."

But before I could formulate an answer, before I could compel my heavy tongue to speak, his mood changed. The intensity of his gaze wavered and his shoulders slumped. His playfulness gave way to something new.

Regret?

He sat back in his seat, looking down at his dogs. "I'm sorry. That was inappropriate."

My heart was still pounding. My palm was sweaty, and I wiped it on my jeans. I had to clear my throat before I could speak. "I think I started it."

He laughed, but it wasn't the way he'd laughed earlier. This laughter had a hard edge to it. "I can't believe I forgot."

"Forgot what?"

He put his head in his hands and rubbed his face, suddenly looking weary. "It's been a long day."

I had no idea what had just happened between us, but I knew when I'd overstayed my welcome. I stood up, and when he looked up at me, I had a feeling he was relieved.

"It was nice meeting you," I said. The words felt inadequate. Utterly mundane.

"You didn't even get a chance to finish your beer."

"Yeah, well." I floundered for something to say. "Maybe another time."

It felt like a stupid thing to say, but he smiled at me anyway. "I'd like that."

I went alone back up the stairs to my porch and stood at the railing of my balcony, looking down at the yard. Bert and Betty were outside now, sniffing among fallen leaves and the dead husks of Regina's flowers. The sky overhead was cloudless, the stars bright and clear. A cool breeze caressed my skin, and for once I didn't care that my left arm was bare.

It was a perfect fall evening, the kind of evening that made every kid think longingly of pumpkin patches and corn mazes and trick-or-treating. But I wasn't thinking of those things. I was thinking of Nick's parting words.

I'd like that.

Chapter Two

THAT NIGHT I dreamed about Nick. I couldn't remember the details when I woke, but I knew it had been about him, and I knew it had been erotic. I was left with a lingering sense of arousal that made me uneasy.

I'd known since I was a teenager that I was attracted to men—I was well past being able to deny it—but somehow I'd never pictured myself in a homosexual relationship. Plenty of gay men married women and made lives for themselves. That was what I wanted, not because I thought homosexuality was a sin, but because I'd already disappointed my mother too many times. First I'd had the bad luck to be born flawed. Later the stutter had developed. Then there'd been high school.

I didn't want to think about that.

It was all in the past anyway. If I settled down and had a family, maybe she'd be proud of me. Maybe having grandchildren would erase the grim scowl from her face.

Of course, in order to marry a woman, I'd actually have to meet one. And date her. I'd have to fall in love.

Hard enough to do without thoughts of Nick Reynolds clouding my brain. And why should I waste my time obsessing about him, anyway? When I'd come home from Nick's apartment the night before, I'd felt almost giddy, but in the cool light of day, the events began to seem far less romantic and far more casual. What had really happened? Nothing. I'd sat in his kitchen with him. I'd drunk half a beer. We'd exchanged pleasantries. Nothing more. Upon closer examination, I was sure he'd never actually been flirting with me. After all, why would he? Nick was gorgeous and confident and could probably have any man—or woman—he set his sights on. And what was I? A one-armed shut-in with borderline social anxiety.

Why would he want me?

By the time I heard him come home from work, I felt like I was back to normal. I found myself missing Regina, whom I'd never even talked to. She'd been the cornerstone of my fantasy. The linchpin in my illusion that my life could ever be normal.

I missed hearing her play.

I went on like that for the better part of a week, alternately obsessing about Nick and doing my best to pretend he didn't exist. I'd see him come and go from work, although I stayed out of sight. Occasionally I saw him in the backyard with his dogs, but I was too scared to go down and talk to him. I wished desperately for him to knock on my door again, to offer me another beer, but he never did. I spent hours debating how I could approach him, planning exactly what I'd say, only to have my courage fail when I had the opportunity to follow through. Then, when the day had ended and the house was quiet both upstairs and down, I lay in bed scolding myself, telling myself I was just lonely, I needed a friend, but that finding a male lover was the last thing on my mind.

Mostly, though, I went about my life as usual, which was to say, I stayed hidden in my home.

When I finally spoke to him again, it was coincidence more than anything. I paid to have my groceries delivered to my front door each week. I requested they be left on my front porch. I paid online and left the driver's tip under the mat. It was all arranged to allow me to avoid the grocery stores, the pointing children, the awkwardness of holding my wallet pinned to my body with my stump while rooting through it with my good hand, the embarrassment of the delivery man who didn't know whether to hand me the groceries or whether to offer to bring them in.

I was just stepping out onto my front porch to retrieve them when Nick arrived home from work. He could have waved, maybe yelled hello and gone on his way around the side of the house to his door, but instead he came up to the porch.

Great. Now, instead of a delivery man, I had Nick to deal with.

"What's all this?" he asked, looking at the bags and boxes at my feet.

"Groceries." I gathered up most of the plastic bags by their handles and draped them over my left arm. My left elbow was intact, and I had nearly two inches of arm below that, so I could hang them from the bend of my stump.

And that's what it was—a stump. Some people preferred the term "residual limb," but to me, that didn't do it justice. It was like changing the diagnosis of "shell shock" to "post-traumatic stress disorder." As if adding more syllables to it could alter the truth of the situation. As if having a longer phrase could make my arm longer too.

I could feel Nick watching me as I looped the bag handles over the crook of my elbow, although it didn't make me as uncomfortable as it usually did. He didn't offer to help either. Most people turned away and pretended not to notice my predicament, or they fell all over themselves trying to do it for me, but Nick just stood there watching. So many times I'd been annoyed at people for helping when it wasn't needed, but now I couldn't help but wonder why he wasn't.

I picked up the last bag in my right hand, leaving only one box.

"I'll get that one," he said.

And in the blink of an eye, I did a one-eighty. I went from being annoyed because he wasn't helping to being annoyed that he was. "You don't have to do that."

He smiled at me, and I had the uncomfortable feeling he knew exactly what I was thinking. "I'm not being charitable. I'm being rude. This way I can walk into your house rather than waiting for you to invite me in." He balanced the box on his left hand and opened the door for me with his right. "After you."

Whether my annoyance was rational or not, he'd managed to derail it. I couldn't be mad, which left me with nothing but nervous butterflies in my stomach.

He followed me in, and without being asked, he began taking groceries out of the bags, setting them on the counter for me to put away. "I haven't seen you," he said.

I was glad I didn't have to face him. Instead, I could concentrate on picking up cans of soup and putting them in the cupboard.

"I've been busy."

"Doing what?"

"Working."

"Where do you work?"

"I work for Here and Now. They're a marketing company. Mostly I design brochures and newsletters and put together postcard advertising campaigns."

"You work from home?"

"Yes."

The groceries were all laid out on the counter now. He leaned back against my table to watch while I sorted through them and put them away.

"You have your groceries delivered."

It wasn't a question. "Yes."

"I notice an awful lot of catalogs in your mailbox."

I stopped, staring down at the boxed entrée in my hand. Our mailboxes were side by side on the front porch, and not deep enough to hide anything as big as a magazine. It was something anybody might have noticed, but it felt like an intrusion.

"So?"

"So I'm beginning to think you don't get out much."

I slammed the cupboard door closed, harder than I'd intended, and turned to face him. I wanted to tell him to mind his own business, but I didn't trust myself to speak. The last thing I wanted was to start stuttering.

He stared back at me, completely unfazed by my discomfort. He pointed at the box in my hand. "That stuff's crap, you know. Too much sodium. Tons of glutamates. No nutritional value whatsoever."

Too fast. Talking to him made my head spin. He was always jumping too quickly from one thing to another, from intimate to casual in the blink of an eye. I looked down at the chicken potpie. "It's kept me alive this long."

He laughed. "Still, I think we can do better. How about if I make you dinner instead?"

He wanted to cook for me?

I cleared my throat, tested the obedience of my tongue, and finally managed to say, "Sounds great."

I'D NEVER been in the basement apartment other than my first visit there with Nick, and even then, we'd gone in the back door, straight from the backyard into the kitchen. I hadn't been able to see much of the living space. I'd always imagined white carpets, sleek black furniture, and warm afternoon light falling through the windows onto Regina's piano.

The reality was quite different. The floors were covered with a mottled brown berber, and the walls sported wood paneling straight out of the seventies. Nick's furniture looked soft and cushy, but was all hidden beneath blankets.

"The dogs aren't supposed to get on the couches, but they do anyway," he told me. "The minute I walk out the door."

Betty, Bert, and Bonny jumped exuberantly around his feet, all of them trying to nose their way to the front. I wandered through the living room into the dining room where I found Regina's piano with two unpacked boxes and a pile of mail on top. I sat down on the bench and lifted the hinged overlay covering the keys. I ran my fingers over them, not playing any notes but feeling the smoothness of the keys. I imagined how it must feel to be able to tease art from such a mundane object.

Nick went past me into the kitchen and came back out with a bottle of mineral water and an open beer. He

placed the latter on the piano in front of me. I stared at
it for a moment, seeing the brown glass and the con-
densation already forming on the outside. "You should
use a coaster."

"Ha!" he laughed. "Wow. Do I look like the kind of
guy who even owns coasters?"

I felt myself blush. "I wouldn't want her piano to
get messed up."

He regarded me for a moment, looking puzzled.
"She left it, you know," he said at last. "It must not have
meant that much to her."

I looked down at my lap, suddenly worried we
weren't talking about the piano anymore. That maybe
he knew my secret, the way I'd tried so hard to convince myself that I could have a life with her. I felt him
watching me. I could almost taste his curiosity.

"Are you going to ask?" I asked.

"Ask what?"

"Why I live like a hermit?"

He cocked his head at me, almost smiling.
"Should I?"

"No."

He shrugged. "I suppose you'll tell me when
you're ready."

"I don't think I'll ever be ready."

"Fair enough."

I took a drink of my beer, not because I wanted it
but because I felt awkward and it gave me something
to do.

"Listen, do you mind if I shower before we eat?
I've been working all day, and I feel kind of gross."

"Sure."

"I'll be out in a flash." He set his mineral water down on the piano. Halfway out of the room, he

stopped short and came back. He pulled an unopened envelope out from his stack of mail and placed it under the bottle of water in lieu of a coaster. He winked at me as he turned away. I was glad he was out of the room and couldn't see me blush.

The water began to run. The sound seemed un-usually loud in the hushed apartment. I pictured him shedding his clothes, climbing into the shower, letting the hot water run down his chest—

Stop.

I took a huge swig of beer, draining at least half the bottle, although it made me cough. I put the remainder down on the envelope next to his water.

Now what?

The piano loomed in front of me, mute and mo-rose. Did it miss Regina? Did it resent being reduced from an instrument of beauty to a glorified coffee table?

I reached out, touching it gently, as if the keys might disintegrate beneath my fingers the way my dream of Regina had. I gently pushed a key. The sound was barely distinguishable above the sound of the run-ning water. I played it again, louder this time. A single note. I didn't know how to play a chord. I didn't know how to add harmony to melody. I could only hit ran-dom keys, a mockery of real music. It made me inex-plicably sad.

It's meant to be played. It won't break.

I hit the key hard this time. At the exact same mo-ment, the water in the bathroom turned off. The note rang out, loud and vibrant, yet still alone. Still in need of accompaniment.

I felt silly, especially when Nick appeared in the doorway wearing sweats and a T-shirt, his hair still wet. "You play?"

Teasing a bit, but there was nothing malicious behind his words, so I laughed. "Yeah. You've now heard
the full extent of my repertoire."

"You should do something about that." He picked
up his bottle of water and headed for the kitchen. "You
can practice while I cook. I'll call you when it's ready."

Within moments the homey sounds of cooking began to fill the kitchen—pots clanging and water running, a knife on a cutting board, the oven door opening
and closing. I sat, comfortably nursing my beer.

And I played the piano.

It wasn't playing the way Regina had played. It
probably wasn't playing by any reasonable definition.
But as the alcohol began to warm me, I grew bold. I
tested the keys, from the solemn low notes to the chirpy
highs. From the bright white keys to the oddly discor-
dant black ones. I played the one song I knew how to
play over and over again—a simple, one-handed version of "Frère Jacques," taught to me by my paternal
grandmother when I was a kid. I should have felt ridiculous, a one-armed man playing piano, but somehow I
knew Nick wouldn't mind.

I knew he wouldn't laugh.

Half an hour later, dinner was ready. He served me
broiled fish, a medley of steamed vegetables, and fresh
fruit salad. I stared at it, wondering for a moment how
insulted he'd be if I went back for my chicken potpie.

"I guess I should have warned you, I'm a bit of a
health nut."

I looked at him, bulging arms and all. "I should
have known."

Although it wasn't the tastiest meal I'd ever eaten,
it was undoubtedly the healthiest one I'd had in ages.
It wasn't until we'd finished eating and I was starting

my third beer that Nick leaned forward on the table, bringing himself closer to me.

"So tell me, Owen. Why do you live like a hermit?"

I'd just taken a drink and I paused, surprised by the question, my mouth full and my beer bottle frozen halfway between my lips and the table. I felt vulnerable. I swallowed hard and set the bottle down carefully, afraid my shaking hand would tip it over. I found myself holding my left arm close to my body, hugging myself with my right arm in an attempt to hide my stump. It was an old habit. It was something my mother had hated. "I thought you were going to wait until I was ready to talk about it."

"I think you are ready. I think that's why you brought it up in the first place." When I looked up at him, I found him slightly amused, but there was no mockery in his eyes. "I've been there, you know. I've shut myself in." It was hard to believe. He seemed so well adjusted. So *normal*, if there was any such thing. But there was no denying the quiet compassion I felt from him. "What is it? Social anxiety disorder?"

It seemed he wasn't about to let me off the hook a second time, so I answered. "Not really. At least, I don't think so."

"So, you've never been diagnosed?"

"No. It's not really that acute. It's not like I panic or anything. It's just something I'd rather not do. It makes me uncomfortable."

"Okay. But *why*?"

"It makes me self-conscious."

"About what?"

"My arm. And my stutter."

His eyebrows went up. "You don't stutter."

"Not often. Not anymore. But when I get nervous, it starts to manifest."

"I see." He leaned back in his seat again, indicating the interrogation was already over and we were returning to less embarrassing topics. "What are you doing tomorrow night?"

"Nothing. Why?"

"There's a new Greek restaurant in town. I hear you get to break plates. Will you come with me?"

My heart skipped a beat. Was he asking me out? Like, on an actual date? "Why?"

"Why do they break plates? I don't know. Must be a Greek thing."

"No, I mean, why are you inviting me?"

He shrugged. "Why not? I get tired of cooking. And I get sick of sitting home alone. I'm guessing you do too."

That was true, but I was still hesitant. As much as I liked being with him, the idea of going out in public made me nervous. "I don't know."

He shifted in his seat, not meeting my eyes, suddenly looking uncomfortable and embarrassed. "I don't mean a date or anything."

Was that why he thought I was balking?

I didn't know how to reassure him that whether or not it was a date really wasn't the issue. Instead, I took a deep breath and asked, "What time?"

Chapter Three

THE FIRST thing Nick did when I opened my front door the next evening was point at my left arm.

"You actually use your prosthetic? My sister always hated hers, although she's talking now about having a mountain bike outfitted for her."

He'd asked a question, but he didn't seem to expect an answer. He was already leading me out the door to his SUV. Still, he'd made me conscious of my prosthetic. My mother had bought it for me when I left for college. I'd wanted something practical like a basic hook, but my mother had always cared more about appearance than my comfort. The fake hand hanging below my cuff looked almost real, but to my mother's dismay, I'd never learned to use it well. Some newer replacement limbs could do amazing things, but mine tended to hang forgotten at my side. Under my long-sleeved shirt, leather straps around my shoulders helped hold it in place. They were also designed to assist in movement, but it was a skill that required practice. Mostly I'd worn it so as not to have an empty sleeve or an unsightly stump for my date with Nick.

Even if it wasn't a date.

I was uncomfortable in the car. The straps around my shoulders felt too tight. It had been so long since I'd worn it, I'd undoubtedly gained weight and hadn't bothered to loosen them. I shifted in my seat, trying to alleviate the pressure across the top of my back. My stump began to itch. I caught Nick glancing sideways at me as I squirmed and fidgeted, and I forced myself to hold still.

This was a terrible idea.

Let's get takeout. Let's go back home.

I wanted to say the words, but I was too much of a coward.

The restaurant was downtown, just past the Light District. The parking lot was full.

"I saw a spot a couple of blocks back. How do you feel about walking?" Nick asked.

"Fine with me."

It was a great night for it, really. The breeze was chilly. Dry leaves skittered before us across the pavement, rustling and crackling. We walked side by side in silence, our footfalls somehow in sync.

The restaurant was a rude awakening. It was packed and absolutely deafening. I used my right hand to hold my prosthetic against my body so I wouldn't bump people with it. We had to stand for a long time, waiting for a table. It was too loud to talk. I felt claustrophobic. I was sure everybody must be looking at my arm, although I was too embarrassed to actually look around and see. I stood there, huddled between Nick and the wall, wishing I had enough nerve to say, "Let's go someplace else." They finally seated us across from each other at a tiny table. Each spot held a dinner plate, a bread plate, flatware, and two glasses, one for water and one for wine. There was also a bottle of olive oil, one of ketchup, salt and pepper, and a flip chart of appetizers and desserts. And a wine list.

"Where the hell is the food going to go?" I asked. There was barely an inch of open space.

"What?" Nick asked, cupping his hand behind his ear.

I sighed and said in a near shout, "It's really loud in here!"

"It is. I had no idea it would be this crowded."

I nodded, unsure what to say. The waitress stopped at our table long enough to pour water and wedge a plate of bread between our glasses. Not sliced bread, but one big hunk with a serrated knife stabbed into the center like some kind of ritual killing. I stared at it, hating it. Why couldn't they bring sliced bread? Had they ever considered how hard it was to slice bread with only one hand?

Of course they hadn't. Why would they?

Nick was already browsing the menu, which was roughly the size of a newspaper. I tried to scoot my chair back to give myself room to open mine without being dangerously close to spilling my water all over the bread, but there was no room behind me to move into.

The waitress stopped at our table, pad and pen in hand, looking frazzled. I suspected her hair had begun the night in a tight twist, but it was now coming loose and falling around her face. She had smudged mascara and a run in her stockings. "Are you ready to order?"

"We'll start with the sampler appetizer," Nick said. "And I'd like a mineral water."

They both turned to me, and I felt my throat begin to clench up. Restaurants were one of my biggest triggers. *"This is the real world,"* my mother used to say. *"You have to be able to interact with people. You'll never get anywhere in life if you can't even order dinner."* My mother always made ordering dinner feel like a test. If I stuttered, I failed. If I didn't stutter? Well, I'd probably find some other way to fail. The night was young and ripe with possibilities.

"Uh…," I said stupidly.

The waitress blew her hair out of her eyes. "House red's on special until seven. Want to try that?"

"Y-yes. Sure. Th-thank you."

"You like wine?" Nick asked when she was gone.

"Not really."

He cocked his head at me in confusion. "Then why did you order it?"

Because it was the easy way out. But what I said was, "I thought I'd try something new."

He seemed to approve of that sentiment. "I don't eat out often. Restaurant food is loaded with sodium and empty calories. But every once in a while it's nice to splurge." He looked down at his menu. "I'm thinking lamb chops or moussaka."

"No broiled fish?"

He laughed. "Definitely not."

I finally managed to open my menu, although I knocked over my wineglass in the process. I counted myself lucky it was still empty. I scanned the menu, thinking less about what sounded good and more about what would be easy to eat. Pasta was always a good bet, as was fish, except we'd had that the night before.

Not steak, because it could be hard to cut. Nothing from the Two-Handed Sandwiches section, although I laughed to myself at the title. At least they'd given me fair warning.

The waitress stopped again to set down our drinks. I'd assumed she'd pour the wine into the glass in front of me, but instead she brought a new one, although she had to carefully rearrange everything on the tabletop to make room for it.

She blew her hair out of her eyes again and pulled her pad and pen out. "You ready?" She didn't even look at us. Her gaze flitted around the room, taking note of what needed to be done next—who needed water refills and who needed their check. She was hurried and weary, and her impatience made me self-conscious in an all-too-familiar way.

Nick ordered—lamb chops *and* moussaka—and then it was my turn. And in that instant, I knew I was doomed. I felt the panic clawing at the back of my throat, making my mouth unresponsive. "I-I-I'd like the b-b-b-b—" I stopped and took a deep breath, feeling their eyes on me. My cheeks burned. I couldn't possibly look at Nick. I kept my eyes on my menu and tried again. "The b-b-b—"

"The bruschetta?" the waitress asked. "Or the baked penne?"

"N-n-no. The b-b-b—" I stopped again. In that moment, I hated her. I hated the damn restaurant. I hated my nerves for making me stutter at the worst possible moments.

"Why don't you give us a minute?" Nick said.

My relief at being granted a reprieve was overshadowed by my embarrassment. "I'm s-s-s-s—" I couldn't even get the word sorry out. The frustration was like a weight in my chest. I had the sudden urge to cry. I tried to stand up, but there was no room to move my chair back, and as I stood, my menu fell forward, knocking over glasses. I reached for them, instinctively, with both arms, but I'd forgotten about my prosthetic. I wore it so seldom, and in my panic, I didn't account for the extra eighteen inches of metal and rubber attached to my stump.

My false hand crashed into the Tetris puzzle that was our tabletop. Wine spilled everywhere. So did Nick's mineral water. Two of the glasses fell to the floor, shattering with a crash that silenced the chaos around us. Everybody turned our way, and I imagined their surprise and their quiet snickers when they saw who was responsible.

"I have to go," I said, without meeting Nick's eye. "I'm s-s-sorry. I j-j-j—"

"Owen?"

He reached across the table for me and I jerked away. I looked up and saw the waitress headed our way with our appetizers, annoyance written all over her face. "I n-n-need to l-leave."

"Okay," he said, his voice calm and reasonable. "Wait for me at the car, okay? Give me a minute to pay the bill."

I nodded, but the only thing that held me to that promise was the fact that I didn't have keys to his SUV and it would have been a long walk home. I'd made a fool of myself, and in front of Nick, no less. I leaned against his vehicle and covered my eyes with my good hand. When I finally heard him approach, I couldn't even look at him.

He stopped directly in front of me, ducking down a bit to try to force me to meet his eyes. "Are you okay?"

No, I wasn't okay. I was a mess. Embarrassed and ashamed. "I'm s-sorry," I blurted out. "Jesus, I'm so sorry!"

"For what? The whole reason we went there was so we could break things."

I thought I heard the smile in his voice, but I couldn't return it. "Still—"

"Owen, stop." He put his fingers under my chin and lifted it, forcing me to face him. To see that he was indeed smiling at me with a kindness that went a long way toward soothing my embarrassment. "You don't need to be sorry. If anything, I should apologize for bullying you into coming out tonight. And I picked the worst possible restaurant. We should have left the minute I saw how crowded it was."

"I feel like a fool."

"Don't," he said simply. "There's no reason."

His easy acceptance of my neurosis only made me feel worse. "I'll pay you back for the wine and whatever else was on the bill."

He waved his hand at me. "Don't worry about it." He gestured down the street toward the Light District. "There's another place we can go. Nothing fancy, but it won't be crowded like that Greek place. It's called the Vibe. Do you know it?"

"No." I didn't know any of the places in town that didn't deliver.

"It's sort of an aging-hippie sandwich joint. Sometimes they have live music in the back. We can walk down there and check it out, and if you don't like it, we'll take the sandwiches to go, okay?"

I could have hugged him for making it so easy on me. "Okay."

But instead of turning to lead me away from the car, he took a step closer to me. "First things first, though." He reached up and pushed my coat off my shoulders.

"I'll freeze without my coat."

"I know." He pulled it free and tossed it onto the hood of his car. "You'll get it back." Then, to my surprise, he began to unbutton my shirt.

"What are you doing?"

"What we should have done before we left the house."

He finished with the buttons and pushed the shirt off my shoulders. I wore a T-shirt underneath it, under the straps that held my arm in place, but it still felt strange to have him remove my shirt. "Undressing me?" I asked. My voice shook. I was painfully aware of how close he stood. Of how good he smelled. Of the gentleness of his hands as he helped me remove my prosthetic from the sleeve. He left my shirt on the hood of his car, just as he'd done with my jacket.

He reached for the buckle on my right shoulder. "Getting rid of this."

I blushed, but I stood still as he undid the strap. He was close enough I could easily have kissed him if I'd dared. He finished the first buckle and began to undo the one on the other side. "I feel silly," I said. Silly and ridiculously aroused, but I opted to keep that latter bit to myself.

"Why?"

"I just do."

"Well, stop." He pushed the straps off my shoulders and reached for my arm, but I pulled back, thinking of the wrapping underneath, of the sweat and the way my skin was always red and inflamed after wearing the prosthetic.

"Don't. You don't want to do that."

"I've done it a hundred times for my sister." He laughed. "Probably more. Anyway, I'm a doctor, remember?"

"I'm not a dog."

"I'm aware of that fact," he said. And then his laughter seemed to fall away and he added, in a quieter voice, "Excruciatingly aware."

I wasn't sure how to take that. I wasn't sure if it was a compliment or an insult or neither. I stood speechless and confused as he carefully released my arm from my prosthetic. He turned away from me to unlock his car, and while he did, I pulled off the rubber sleeve that fit over my stump. He took that from me too and tossed it like a discarded sock into the back seat of his SUV with my arm. I stood there shivering, watching him, wondering about his sudden change in mood. Wondering if he knew how intimate the past few minutes had felt to me. If he did, he gave no indication. He smiled at me. "Aren't you freezing?"

"As a matter of fact, I am." He waited while I put my shirt back on and rolled my left sleeve up to the base of my stump so it wouldn't flap loose while I walked.

"Do you want me to do the other side to match?" he asked. Blunt and honest, yet practical, since I couldn't roll it up myself.

"No. I'm warmer like this."

Once I had my coat back on, with the left sleeve hiked up to match my shirt, we walked up the street again, but the other way this time. The sandwich shop was infinitely better than the Greek place. It was small but well lit, filled with plants and fish tanks. Small tables sat half-hidden in intimate corners.

Nick gestured toward the counter. "I can order for us if you want to pick a table."

I was touched once again by his sensitivity. He was allowing me a chance to hide rather than deal with any of the employees. "Something with turkey," I said.

He smiled at me, causing my stomach to do somersaults. "You got it."

He brought us identical sandwiches, although he had carrot sticks instead of french fries. Always the healthier option. It was no wonder he looked so good.

"I'm sorry about the restaurant."

I couldn't believe he was apologizing to me. I was the one who'd made a scene. "It wasn't your fault."

"No." He shifted uncomfortably in his seat. "I mean, I'm sorry about when you tried to order. I've never seen you struggle with your speech before, and I wasn't sure if I should stop you and order for you or if it was better to let you work it out."

Blunt and honest. I was beginning to get used to it. "It depends a lot on how the listener responds. When they get impatient, like the waitress, it m-makes it harder for me to speak clearly. Once p-people start to notice it, it's l-like it takes on a life of its own."

"Why didn't you just point to what you wanted?"

Such a simple question, and it brought me up short. Why hadn't I? My mother had never allowed that. *"You have to learn to deal with these things, Owen, not run from them."* But still, my mother wasn't here. It was the most obvious solution, so why hadn't it occurred to me? "I guess I just panicked."

"You told me the stutter used to be worse. What happened? Did you do some kind of therapy?"

I swallowed hard and took a long drink of my soda, trying to decide how much to reveal. He waited, patient as a stone. I took the easy way out and said, "A bit, yeah."

"And is that why you get nervous around people?"

"It doesn't help, but the real reason is my arm."

"You don't seem uncomfortable with me, though."

"You're different."

"Why?"

It was a simple question, but the answer was complex. Because he was patient. Because he was direct yet not insensitive. Because he never laughed at me, and he made me feel safe. What I ended up saying was, "Because you aren't weirded out by it."

"And others are?"

"You said your sister has the same defect—"

"Don't call it a defect. It's a congenital amputation."

"Fine. My point is, you've probably seen how people act. The way kids always ask about it—"

"And that bothers you?"

"It's not the kids themselves who annoy me. They don't know any better, and it's natural for them to ask questions. It's the way their parents hush them up and rush away, like they can pretend I don't exist. Kids may be the most vocal, but adults are the worst."

"How so?"

"They either get so flustered trying to help with every little thing that I end up feeling like an invalid, or they do their best to ignore it altogether, like they somehow don't notice that I'm missing an arm."

He cocked his head at me in puzzlement. "How do you want them to act?"

"I don't know. Normal, I guess. I want them to act like I'm not a freak."

He shifted carrot sticks around in his basket, thinking. "You know, most people are trying to treat you the way they think you want to be treated."

"They think I want to be treated like a pariah?"

He looked up at me with a piercingly direct gaze. "Owen, this isn't high school. Most people are genuinely good. They don't want to be cruel."

I ducked my head, feeling like a recalcitrant child. In alluding to high school, he'd hit the proverbial nail on the head. All of my insecurities went back to my teen years, but most adults didn't act the way teenagers did. And yet, I knew how adults acted too. I knew the way they forced smiles and turned away.

He went on, unaware of my turmoil. "When people meet you, they're not sure how to behave. That's true. Look at the whole handicapped versus handicapable debate. Or even better, look at how I handled your stutter at the restaurant. It's the same thing. If somebody offers to help, they worry they're treating you like an invalid. If they don't offer to help, then they worry they're being insensitive. If they see you struggling with something, they don't know if you want assistance or if you want to do it yourself. They don't know if they should acknowledge that your arm is missing or not. They worry they're being politically incorrect, and God knows that'll get you crucified in this day and age. But more importantly, they worry they'll offend you. And so they do the only thing they can think to do—they pretend not to notice, because it's better to be oblivious than to be uncaring."

I sat in silence, weighing his words, trying to look at it from somebody else's point of view.

"I'd like you to meet my sister. She handles these things differently than you."

"Better, you mean."

He shrugged. "No, not necessarily. She can be a bit extreme. But she might help you get a bit of perspective." He shrugged again, smiling. "Look, you're fine. I was just making conversation, not trying to force you to reevaluate your outlook on life, you know? You don't need to meet her. You don't need to change a damn thing. I'm only trying to help." He winked at me. "But only if you want it."

Chapter Four

TWO DAYS later I met June. She was shorter than Nick and me by several inches, with wild, dark brown hair flying around her head in crazy, wiry curls. The only thing that gave her away as Nick's sister was her eyes. They were identical to Nick's.

"Hey, big brother," she said. And then she turned to me. "You must be Owen." She waved her shortened right arm at me. "Look at us! Aren't we a pair?"

She was like a whirlwind in the small apartment, petting the dogs, talking a hundred miles a minute, playing Annoying Little Sister to Nick's Stern Big Brother to a tee. I was immediately aware of the way she used her amputated arm. She gestured with it. She used it to smack Nick in the arm, to adjust the headband that held her hair out of the way, to hold the beer Nick handed her. My mother had always encouraged me not to use it because using it drew attention to it. *"For Christ's sake, Owen,"* she'd say, *"use your* good *arm! Do you want everybody to stare?"* When I wore long-sleeved shirts, she'd tuck my cuff into my pocket, as if people might not realize something was wrong with my arm. As if they'd think I was standing with my hand in my pocket. But every time she did it, I'd end up trying to use my arm and pulling the sleeve free, and then she'd cringe at the way it flapped loose at my side.

I watched June using her arm like anybody would, and I felt a twinge of sadness. But mostly I felt angry. I'd always known my mother was embarrassed by my arm, but for some reason it had never occurred to me to blame her for that fact. I'd always subscribed to her view that I'd wronged her, or at the very least, that the universe and biology had wronged her. But I'd never blamed her. Even when I'd realized that most of my stuttering seemed to hinge upon her and her reaction to it, I hadn't ever felt she was in the wrong.

Why was that? Partly because some of what she did really was for my own good, like insisting I learn to type. But some of her lessons had felt downright cruel. I still had a hard time facing her.

Nick and June were still talking, discussing some cousin who had come home from college pregnant, and I found myself back at Regina's piano, idly playing as I contemplated my relationship with my mother until June bounced in and sat on the bench next to me.

"Teach me," she said.

"I d-don't know how to play."

"You were playing when I came in."

I blushed. "Just 'Frère Jacques.' It's the only song I know."

"So?" she said as if it were inconsequential. "Teach me."

I showed her the song, but sitting side by side as we were, with our good arms together, our hands were too close on the keyboard. She got up and moved to sit on my left. "Between us, we make a whole player," she said, not as if it bothered her but as if she found it amusing.

We played "Frère Jacques" over and over again until we were in sync.

"You guys might want to consider broadening your repertoire," Nick said from his place on the couch. "That song's getting old really fast."

"You know any songs, hotshot?" she asked.

"There's music in the bench."

June and I looked at each other, intrigued. Without saying a word, we both stood up and turned to lift the lid. The inside was full of music books.

"Intermediate, intermediate, intermediate," June mumbled as she looked through them. "Aha! This one says beginner."

We closed the bench and sat back down, side by side. She put the book in front of us and opened it to a page in the middle. We leaned closer to study it.

"Damn," she said. "Somehow I thought beginner would be a bit easier than this." She looked over at me. "You know how to read music?"

"Sort of. I did two years of band in junior high."

"Me too!" she said. "What did you play?"

I held up my right hand. My *only* hand. "Guess."

She put her finger on her chin, tipping her head as she thought. "Either trumpet or percussion."

"Not even percussion, per se. Bass drum. On every single song." With only one hand, I hadn't ever been able to play the snare drum or timpani well enough to beat out the other kids. "I did get to play bells on a couple of the easy songs. But 90 percent of the time, it was bass drum. I got tired of doing nothing but hitting that big drum every first and third beat. How about you? What did you play?"

She held up her one good hand and wiggled her fingers. "French horn."

Behind us, Nick snorted. "Yeah, she made this huge stink about being allowed to play. Talked my parents into buying her her own horn. Then she quit after only two years."

"Brass instruments are gross," she said, more to me than to him. "I gagged every time I had to clear the spit valve." She pointed to one of the notes in the open book. "I know this is a C."

"Every Good Boy Does Fine," I recited, pointing to the treble clef.

"The spaces in the bass clef are All Cars Eat Gas."

We both looked up at the piano in front of us. "So which one's C?" I asked.

She shrugged. "Hell if I know."

I slumped, feeling defeated, although I couldn't have said why. It wasn't as if I'd expected to pull out music and be able to play it. Still….

"Hey!" June said. "We should take lessons together like this! You playing right hand and me playing left. How hard can it be?"

Pretty fucking hard, was my first thought. "Are you serious?"

"Why not?"

"That's enough," Nick said, standing up from his spot on the couch. "Let's go out to dinner before you try to recruit Owen for the London Symphony Orchestra."

"Killjoy," she said, but she dropped the subject.

I hadn't thought ahead to how it would be at the restaurant, June and I both walking in together. The hostess did a fast double take but quickly recovered. It was the young man who showed us to our table who couldn't seem to stop staring. June looked right at him as we sat down. Her gaze was as piercing as Nick's often was.

"Shark attack," she said. She pointed at me. "Him too."

The kid's eyes widened. He looked back and forth between us, probably trying to decide how seriously to take her. "Really? Like, the same shark?"

She snorted in disgust. "Of course not. Have you ever seen a shark that could eat two arms at once?" She shook her head at Nick. "Can you believe this guy?"

The kid turned scarlet and fled. I wondered if my cheeks were as red as his.

"Knock it off," Nick said to June.

"He started it."

We managed to order without incident. It wasn't until our salads came that June leaned forward on the table to look at me. Her actions and her gaze were so much like Nick's, it unnerved me. "You know what keeps me up at night?"

I looked at Nick for help. He was giving me a look that said, "You're on your own." I turned back to June. "I have no idea," I confessed.

"Wondering if I'm actually right-handed."

I looked down at her amputated right arm, which held her weight on the table. In her left hand, she held her fork over her salad bowl. "Are you serious?"

"Think about it. Hand dominance isn't learned. It's genetic, and only about 10 percent of people are left-handed. And this." She pointed with her fork toward her shortened arm. "Depending on which source you're looking at, the statistics for ABS are anywhere from one in twelve hundred to one in fifteen hundred. That means the chances that I'm actually left-handed are roughly one in thirteen thousand."

"That's not how probability works," Nick said.

She ignored him completely and pointed to my right hand. "You have way better odds than me."

I looked down at my right hand, suddenly appreciating it more than I had before. "I guess that never occurred to me."

"She used that little ploy to talk our parents into the best prosthetic money could buy, back in junior high," Nick said to me. "Then she quit wearing it three months later."

"Not completely."

"Close enough."

"It was heavy!"

"Yes, I know. You whined about it every five minutes."

It was strange to me, the way they could bicker, and yet it was obvious they loved each other. I didn't think Nick was actually as annoyed at her as he pretended to be, and she didn't seem to take anything he said to heart anyway.

"What do you miss most?" she asked me over our entrees. "I mean, of the things you can't do, which one really drives you crazy?"

"I wish I could hammer a nail. All of my walls are blank because I can't put in nails to hold up pictures." She nodded in understanding, and I found myself laughing. It was a ridiculous conversation, but I asked anyway, "What do you miss?"

"I want to be able to hold my morning coffee the way they always do in commercials, you know? With both hands wrapped around it so the cup can make your fingers warm and you don't have to use the handle."

Such a simple thing, to hold a coffee cup. For the first time, I saw a hint of anger in Nick's eyes, not directed at his sister, but at the unfairness of life.

"I've never thought about that," I admitted.

"You'll never be able to drink coffee and *not* think about it, now."

As we were leaving the restaurant, she bumped my amputated arm playfully with hers. "You doing anything for Halloween?"

"Not that I know of."

"Want to come to a party with me? We can tape our stumps together and tell everyone we're conjoined twins, attached at the forearm."

"No, thanks."

"It'll be fun," she said. "I'll talk you into it later. And I'll find us a piano teacher too."

Was she serious? She skipped ahead of us, and I slowed down to fall into step with Nick. He put his arm around my shoulders. Such a simple, friendly gesture, but it made my heart race. He leaned close as if he were about to share a secret with me. "She's a force to be reckoned with."

"I'm starting to figure that out."

"Welcome to my life."

"Does she ever *not* get her way?"

"Not often enough, Owen. Not often enough."

"WAS SHE always like that?" I asked Nick after June had gone. We were back in the comfort of my own apartment, and although I'd liked Nick's sister, I was glad she'd left.

"Always. My mom says she came out of the womb determined to make the world pay her back for her missing hand." He laughed, thinking about it. "When she was three or four, she'd imitate Captain Hook. She'd say, 'I'll fight you with one arm behind my back!' But then she'd put her good arm behind her back and brandish her stump. It never seemed to occur to her to do it the other way."

"Maybe she really is right-handed."

"You know what she dressed as for Halloween when we were kids?"

"What?"

"A superhero. Almost every year. Wonder Woman was her favorite, but there was also Batgirl, Spider-Man, and Superman." He ticked them off on his fingers. "Oh. And one year we were the Wonder Twins."

"When I was in third grade, I dressed up as Superman, but when I was getting ready for trick-or-treating, my mom said, 'Not sure what good a one-armed hero is.' So I didn't go."

The minute I said it, I regretted it because he immediately turned serious. "Your mom *said* that to you?"

I blushed and turned away. "It doesn't matter."

"Like hell it doesn't."

"It's no big deal. My dad took me to a movie instead." But I'd never asked to dress up as a superhero again. In fact, I'd quit dressing up for Halloween completely after that. "Anyway," I said, wanting desperately to change the subject and get back to the playful banter of before, "your sister's a trip. I can see why you wanted me to meet her."

"Don't read too much into it. I also meant it when I said she can be extreme."

"Like the shark thing?"

"Not that so much. But sometimes she refuses to accept that she's different. I mean, I understand her reasoning, but it's not always about being equal."

"Like what?"

"Well, like when she was a sophomore in high school. She'd been playing soccer up until then, but suddenly that year, she decided she was going to play volleyball instead. Now, don't get me wrong. Maybe there's somebody out there with only one arm who can still play volleyball well, but I'm here to tell you, it wasn't her. But she insisted. She made such a stink about how they were excluding her that the school finally caved and told the coach he had to put her on the team. Susan Granger got cut, even though she was a far better player than June, all because my sister had to prove a point."

"Wow."

"Exactly. And then she quit a year later. Went back to playing soccer instead."

I thought back to eighth grade, when I'd signed up for soccer. I played for half a year before my mother suggested I concentrate on not letting my stump flap around so much as I ran. My father bought me a skateboard, as if that could make up for it, but I never set foot on a soccer field again.

It was unnerving how much my life seemed to mirror June's, and yet in every case, I had the dark, scary, nightmare version.

"Have you noticed the moon tonight?" Nick asked suddenly.

The change of subject surprised me. He was staring out my sliding glass door, and he reached out to me. "Come look," he said as his fingers touched my arm.

Such a simple gesture, but it caused me to freeze in my tracks. Nobody ever touched my left arm. Not

casually, at any rate. Sure, doctors had touched me
there with cold, practical efficiency. And my mother
had touched me there, but only out of embarrassed ne-
cessity. Friends or relatives occasionally, but always by
accident. They always apologized for it, quickly turning away. But in twenty-eight years, I couldn't recall
anybody touching me there the way Nick was touching
me now. I felt the need to hold perfectly still lest he
realize he was touching my ruined arm and pull away.

His fingers moved again, a tickle on my flesh, a
spark of energy that raced up my arm, over my shoulder, and raised goose bumps on the back of my neck.
I shivered, suddenly transported back to a day from
my childhood: sitting in the cold, prickly grass in the
shade of a tree, the buzz of a distant lawnmower, traffic
passing on the street, and me, enthralled by a ladybug
crawling on my left arm. The almost imperceptible kiss
of sensation as it crept down my biceps, over the inside
of my elbow, around the pink apex of my stump, which
was rife with nerve endings and exquisitely sensitive.
That tiny, beautiful bug was oblivious to the horror beneath her feet. My left arm was as good as my right as
far as she was concerned. In my whole life, no person
had ever touched me like that, as if unaware that my left
arm wasn't normal.

Until Nick.

"Owen?" he asked. His hand shifted. Not pulling
away, but changing from a brush of fingers to a gentle
grip around my biceps. "Are you okay?"

I opened my eyes, like waking from a dream, to
find him staring at me. My vision blurred.

"I've upset you. What did I do?"

Jesus, I was crying! I turned away, trying desperately to wipe my eyes. "It's n-n-n—" And now I was

stuttering too. As if I needed a reason to be more embarrassed. "It's nothing."

"It's not nothing. Tell me what I did."

"I'm fine. I'm s-sorry. Must be s-something in my eye." God, was that really the best I could do?

"Owen?"

I felt his hand on my arm again, sliding downward toward the hideous joint of my elbow, and I pulled away, suddenly horrified. "Please," I said, holding up my arms to ward him off, but that only served to draw attention to the fact that one was longer than the other. I looked at the stump of my left arm, pointed obscenely in his direction, and hurried to tuck it back down out of sight at my side. I tried to turn away, but I'd gone as far as I could. I was against the wall, and there he was, staring at me, his eyes wide—not with horror, but with compassion and confusion. I wiped furiously at my eyes. I forced my tongue to move without betraying me. "I'm sorry."

"Don't be sorry. Just tell me what I did."

How could I explain it? Talk of soccer and superheroes had left me raw, and something as simple as his hand on my arm had apparently done me in. "It's n-not your fault."

"But—"

"Give me a m-minute, okay?"

"Sure."

And he did. He took a step back to give me space. I didn't have to look at him to know he was still watching me, patiently waiting for me to get my shit together and stop acting like a freak. Waiting for me to get my traitorous tongue under control. I took a couple of deep breaths. I dried my cheeks. My heart had at least stopped racing. I wasn't as flustered, which meant I could speak clearly. "I'm being stupid. It's really no big deal—"

He reached out again and put his hand on my left shoulder, cutting my words short. For half a second I found myself wondering why he kept touching the left side of my body, but then I realized it was obvious—he was right-handed. And unlike most people, his discomfort at my disability didn't overcome his natural inclination to use his dominant hand.

"Owen?" he asked again.

He was so earnest and reassuring, and I blurted out the answer without realizing I was going to do it. "Nobody touches me."

He pulled his hand away, looking stricken. "You're saying you don't like to be touched?"

"No." And suddenly the absurdity of the situation hit me. I laughed. It felt good, such a normal, healthy release of tension, but it made Nick look even more confused than before. "My arm," I said, gesturing with my right hand toward it. "People don't touch it."

He blinked at me, processing that, and I saw comprehension dawn.

Now that the moment had passed, I was left with nothing but embarrassment that I'd overreacted, and in such a dramatic fashion. "I'm being stupid."

"It's not stupid," he said. He put his hand up again, slower this time, and brushed his fingertips over my upper arm. "Our skin is our largest sensory organ. Humans don't just want to be touched. We *need* it. Babies who aren't touched enough don't thrive. Adults need it too. Wanting to be touched isn't stupid. It's normal." He stroked my arm again. Not a mere touch this time. It was a caress. "What is our flesh for if not to feel?"

Suddenly embarrassment was the last thing on my mind. There wasn't much space left between us, but he managed to move closer. My mouth went dry. I wondered if he could hear my heart pounding.

He stroked both of my arms. His smile turned from gentle and soothing to something that made the blood in my veins rush quickly toward my groin. He leaned forward and kissed my jaw, causing my breath to catch in my throat. His lips teased toward my ear. "The question is," he said, his voice low and husky, "where else haven't you been touched lately?"

I whimpered because it was all I could do. The implication of his words made me dizzy. My cock tried to burst from my jeans. His left arm snuck behind me, around my waist. He ran the fingers of his right hand down my stomach. I put my good arm around his neck, moaning as his fingers reached the buttons on my jeans, anticipating where he'd touch me next, aching desperately for it, wondering without alarm if I'd come in my jeans before he got them undone. I didn't care if I did. All those years of telling myself I could be straight if only I met the right woman were suddenly revealed for sheer folly. I didn't want the right woman. I wanted a man.

I wanted Nick.

He kissed my neck. His erection pushed against mine. It sent a tremor through me, knowing he was as turned on as I was. He slid his hand inside my jeans to cup my groin, and I moaned, arching into him, panting with impatience, ready to give every inch of myself to him. No matter that I was a virgin. No matter that I had no idea what to do. Whatever he wanted, I was ready for it.

Desperate for it.

But then he stopped.

I waited, my heart pounding, my cock straining for more of his touch. Nick took a deep, shuddering breath. He moved his hand away from my groin.

"Nick?" I asked in a hoarse whisper.

He put his forehead on my shoulder. He didn't let me go, but his grip loosened. He put both of his hands on my hips, allowing a tiny gap to grow between us. "I'm sorry." His voice was so soft, I almost didn't hear him.

"Please don't stop."

"I have to."

"I don't understand."

"I know."

And yet he offered no explanation. I could only come up with one possibility. "Is it me?"

His laugh was full of bitterness. "That depends on how you look at it."

That stung, and I took my arm from around his neck, wishing I could pull away, but I was still trapped against the wall.

He must have sensed my dismay, and he stepped back to meet my eyes. It wasn't disgust or shame I saw there, but grief. It made me want to hold him and comfort him, even though I had no idea what was going on.

He cupped my cheek in his hand. "No, Owen. I didn't mean it that way. It's not your fault. I suppose I could blame you for being so damn tempting. All I can think about is how much I want to touch you...."

My world seemed to spin. I was tempting? I was all he could think about? "Then what's the problem?"

"I can't." He kissed my forehead. A quick, tender gesture that made my throat ache. "Good night, Owen." And before I could respond, before I could even catch my breath, he let me go.

And he left.

Chapter Five

THE NEXT few days were torture. I didn't see Nick at all, although I couldn't stop thinking about him or about how perfect it had felt when he touched me. It had been only a few short minutes, and yet in that time, I felt as if all my insecurities had disappeared. For those brief moments, I'd felt brave and sexy.

I'd felt whole.

And yet now I was afraid to face him. I was afraid of what I might see in his eyes.

On the fifth day, June appeared at my door. "I found us a teacher. She'll be here in twenty minutes."

I could only blink at her in surprise. I'd all but forgotten her idea of taking piano lessons. I certainly hadn't expected her to appear on my front porch having already lined up an instructor.

"What if I'm busy?"

"But you're not, are you? Nick says you work from home. That means you're available."

I wanted to be annoyed at her and her wild dark hair and her cocky grin, but what good would it do? Instead I went like a condemned man down the steps to Nick's place.

"Her name's Amelia. Like Amelia Bedelia. Remember those books?"

"No."

"She's going to come twice a week, Mondays and Thursdays at five thirty. Lessons are an hour long. We'll split the cost, okay?"

Did I have a choice?

"She has a recital scheduled the week before Christmas. She asked if we wanted to play in it, and I told her—"

"No!"

"—yes."

"We haven't even learned a note yet!"

"Well, so what? She says lots of her beginning students will be playing in it."

"Oh God," I moaned. The recital was two months away, and already I could feel my blood pressure climbing. I wondered if I could appeal to Nick to talk June out of it.

Of course, that would mean facing him.

He came in from the kitchen to greet me, looking self-conscious and nervous. "I'm glad you came. I was afraid you wouldn't want to see me."

I looked over at June, who was riffling through the music in the piano bench. I stepped closer to Nick and spoke quietly, giving us a semblance of privacy. "Given how we left things, it seems more likely that *you* wouldn't want to see *me*."

He sighed, looking down at the floor. "I'm sorry about what happened."

I could accept the apology, but I wanted more. I wanted to know what had gone wrong. "You mean you're sorry you left?"

"I'm sorry I let myself get carried away like I did."

Not what I wanted to hear, and I still had no idea why he'd chosen to leave me with a bad case of blue balls.

"Are you mad?" he asked.

"Not mad so much as confused."

"I don't blame you." But still, he didn't offer an explanation. He smiled weakly at me. "Friends, right?"

Is that my only option? But what I said was, "Of course." I wondered if he could hear the disappointment in my voice.

He gestured toward June. "I'm sorry about this too. I managed to talk her out of the conjoined twins Halloween costume, but she had her heart set on learning piano."

"The lessons are one thing. It's the recital that has me scared to death."

"You'll do great." The doorbell rang, and June ran into the living room to answer it. Nick gestured toward the kitchen. "I'm just starting to make dinner. Will you stay? Maybe we can watch the Monday night football game?"

I didn't know the first thing about football, but I had nothing better to do, and no matter what had happened between us, he was still the only friend I had. "I'd like that."

"I'LL ADMIT, I've never taught students jointly like this before," Amelia said to June and me at the beginning of the lesson. She was in her early fifties and wore her slate-gray hair in a tight knot on top of her head. Her speech was as careful and as proper as her hair. "The fact that you've both studied music before, however briefly, will be a great help. Learning rhythm can be one of the greatest obstacles for adults, but you already know the basics. The notes will be easy as well. The challenge will be learning to work together. Even the most advanced students sometimes struggle with tempo, especially when they reach a difficult passage in the music, but the two of you will also have to worry about matching each other's tempo."

June and I sat side by side on the piano bench. Amelia sat next to us on a chair Nick had dragged in from the kitchen. "Can it be done?" I asked. "Or are we kidding ourselves?"

For the first time, she smiled, and the effect was extraordinary. In the blink of an eye, she went from unforgiving schoolmarm to some kind of nurturing great-aunt. "It can certainly be done. Every musician who's ever played a duet has struggled with it, and that's really what we're talking about here, isn't it? You'll be playing as a duet. But it will require patience and practice."

Her little speech inspired me. All along I'd been thinking of us as two broken people trying to play piano together, trying to pretend we were one whole pianist, but her view of it was far more practical. Duets were common.

Normal, even.

The first lesson mostly consisted of review— counting time, key signatures, notes. She left us each with a deck of flash cards and a primer book for adults, which was radically different from the beginner books we'd found in the bench. She also showed us a few different pieces we could play in the recital.

"You're not ready to play any of these today, of course, but you may as well pick a song. That way you can start to become familiar with the fingering, and we'll know what to concentrate on."

In the end, June and I selected Beethoven's "Ode to Joy." "A good choice," Amelia said. "A standard for beginning students. It has a nice, simple tempo but a bright, uplifting sound."

Finally, it ended, and we were advised to practice daily. I had Nick's piano, and June assured me she'd buy an electronic keyboard, but we'd also have to arrange to practice together on occasion.

"Just think of it," June said when Amelia was gone. "Today, 'Ode to Joy.' Tomorrow, Carnegie Hall."

I SPENT a great deal of time at Nick's apartment over the next couple of weeks. I practiced relentlessly until I began to worry I'd drive Nick insane.

"Don't be silly," he said when I mentioned it. "I like listening to you."

"How can you like it? I can barely even play songs." Mostly it was finger exercises and scales, and even those I stumbled on more often than not.

"Maybe I like having you here," he said, his gaze flirtatious and direct.

I blushed furiously, but I loved hearing it.

He gave me a key and told me I could practice during the day while he was at work, but I rarely did. I chose to spend those hours attending to my own day job. Besides, practicing after he came home gave me an excuse to be with him. He fed me dinner more often than not. Despite having taken me to the Greek restaurant, he preferred cooking his own meals because he had no control over what restaurants put in his food.

A bit eccentric maybe, but it dovetailed well with my reluctance to go to crowded restaurants. After dinner, we'd take his dogs for a walk, and then we'd settle on the couch for an hour or two of TV before I went home. It was simple, but it was my favorite part of the day. He was always patient and understanding. I was comfortable with him in a way I'd rarely been with anybody.

"Tell me about your stutter," he said one night. We were sitting on the back porch, watching the dogs play in the yard. The sky was beginning to darken, an orange glow appearing in the west. It was chilly, but we were warm and comfortable in our jackets.

"What about it?"

"I'm curious, that's all. You mentioned once that it used to be bad, and yet except for that time at the restaurant, I've barely noticed it."

"It's better than it used to be."

"Because of some kind of therapy?"

I'd intentionally avoided that question the first time he'd asked it, but it seemed dishonest to do it again. "Partly I've learned to deal with it. To talk a bit slower and to anticipate what might trip me up."

"And what's the other part?"

I sighed and hugged my arms around myself, more for comfort than for warmth. "The w-worst thing is feeling like somebody is focusing on me, waiting for me."

"Like the waitress."

"Yes. Restaurants were always the worst. My m-m-mother would force me to order, but she h-hated if I stuttered. She'd say, 'Try to sound normal this time.'"

"You mother said that? She actually implied that you're somehow *not* normal?"

"W-well, I'm not. Sh-she was trying to help." Even if her idea of helping had often made things worse. I didn't want to try to explain it, but I'd inadvertently stumbled into the heart of the issue anyway: my mother.

Nick stared at me, clearly confounded. I had no doubt he would have given my mother a piece of his mind if she'd been present. I wondered if I'd feel vindicated or embarrassed.

I took a deep breath to steady myself. I reminded myself that this was Nick I was talking to. Nick, who would never laugh at me, or roll his eyes, or tell me to spit it out already. Nick, who was my one true friend.

"The stuttering was my m-mother's fault," I said at last. "It's generally accepted that there's a cause, whether it's physiological or psychological. There's some debate about the specifics. I can't really speak for others, but for myself, it's turned out to be largely psychological."

"I don't know if I understand. There must be a physical cause."

"Well, there probably is something that starts it. But how much it continues depends a lot on other factors. One thing that's generally accepted is that anxiety can aggravate it, and the reaction of the listener can aggravate it, which in turn causes more anxiety and more stuttering."

"A vicious cycle."

"Exactly. So, things like having the waitress f-focus on me, and knowing she's imp-p-patient, that can trigger it."

"You're talking about the waitress, but you said it was your mother's fault."

"Yes."

"Because she handled it poorly?"

"She wanted me to be like everybody else. She wanted a normal son."

"Owen, I wish you wouldn't use that word. You *are* normal."

I nodded because I didn't trust myself to speak. On some level I knew he was right. A congenital amputation didn't mean I was *ab*normal. A stutter didn't either. My father had told me the same thing over and over again: *"There's not a damn thing wrong with you, son."* My mother had wanted the best for me, but she'd also wanted me to hide the severed arm that set me apart. And in pushing me to be "normal," she'd often resorted to tactics that had felt almost cruel. No mother would ever do that, people sometimes said. Except I knew the truth. Mothers could do a lot of terrible things in the name of "helping."

"The p-p-point is, it varies a lot from person to person. But for me, my mother is my biggest trigger. High school was the worst, because she'd tell all of my teachers about it, like she was setting me up. And kids would make fun of me. And then…." I stopped there. I wasn't about to share that part of my story yet. "Anyway, around my junior year, my father and I began to notice how much better my speech was when she wasn't around. Coming here for college was the best decision I ever made. I did a bit of speech therapy, but the real solution was getting far away from my mom."

"I don't even know what to say to that. Jesus. Your mother sounds like a real peach."

I shrugged. "What c-c-can I do? We don't get to choose our relatives."

It was as if by speaking of my mother, I manifested her. Only two days later, my parents called.

At first, only my father was on the line. "We haven't heard from you in ages, son. We miss you."

I wondered if his "we" was intentional or acciden-tal. "I miss you too, Dad."

"How's Colorado?"

"Good."

"How's work?"

"About the same."

"Come on, now. Don't give me the short answers. There must be something interesting you can tell me."

I found myself smiling, excited to be able to share my news. "I'm learning piano."

"Really? What brought that on?"

"Well, my friend Nick has one, and his sister talked me into taking lessons with her."

"Oh no," he teased. "A girl talked you into it, huh? Sounds like love to me."

"It's really not like that." Funny, too, how it had never even occurred to me. I'd been too focused on Nick. "She has a congenital amputation of the arm too."

He was quiet for a second, contemplating that. "Well, I'll be damned," he said at last. "That must be quite a sight."

"I think we're playing in a recital in December."

"Perfect timing, then. Your mom and I were thinking about coming down for a visit, just before Christmas."

In the blink of an eye, my happiness at talking to him burned up and blew away like ash in the Colorado wind. "Wh-why?"

"Well—"

He was interrupted by a click as somebody picked up a second line, and then my mother said, "Owen?"

I took my time answering in hopes of keeping my tongue under control. "Hi, Mom."

"I don't suppose you're coming for Thanksgiving."

"N-no, probably not." I hadn't spent a holiday with my mother in four years. I had no intention of starting again now.

"The least you could have done is call and tell me."

"I'm s-sorry."

She sighed, a sudden loud exhale that gave me a clear picture of her face, her eyebrows a sharp V above her eyes, her lips pursed in disapproval. "The neighbors ask, you know, and I have to tell them that my own son doesn't want to come home."

"It's hard to get time off around the holidays," my dad said, coming to my rescue. "And we'll be there in December anyway, Val, so no reason for him to use his PTO. What day is your recital, Owen?"

I managed not to groan, but I knew what was coming. My mother was like a bloodhound, sniffing out anything that might humiliate me. Any glimmer that I might fail at something and embarrass myself more.

"What recital?" she asked.

"Owen's learning to play piano." I wondered if they were standing in the same room, phones pressed to their ears, facing each other across the kitchen as we talked, or if my dad was at the other end of the house, avoiding her as I'd always done.

My mother snorted. "With only one hand?"

"He's taking lessons with a girl who has the same birth defect."

"It's a congenital amputation," I said, hearing Nick's voice in my head.

"We know, Owen," my mother said, sounding exhausted. "So is that what the recital is? Adults with disabilities?"

"N-n-no, M-Mom! It's a r-regular piano recital. W-we're playing a d-duet, th-that's all."

"I hope you don't have to give a speech or any-thing first."

"Wh-wh-why w-would I have to give a sp-speech at a piano recital?"

"Don't be argumentative. I only meant that it's bad enough to have everybody see you walk up there with only one arm, as if you can play as well as them. At least they won't hear you stutter too."

I hung my head, biting my lip to keep from speak-ing because it would never come out right anyway. Her scorn and disgust made my heart pound and my tongue heavy.

"Owen," my dad said, "I know you'll do great. I can't wait to hear you play."

"Th-thanks, Dad," I said. And then, because I knew I couldn't stand to hear my mother say another word, I said, "I have to go now, okay? I'll t-talk to you later."

But ending the call didn't change the horrible weight in my chest or the ache in my throat. I was tempted to climb into bed. To let the weight of my de-pression bear me down, but then I heard one of Nick's dogs bark in the backyard, and I knew what I wanted.

It had been a long time since I'd been so nervous knocking on Nick's door.

"What's wrong?" he asked the minute he let me in. "You look upset."

I nodded. I tried to speak, but my mother was still there in my head, making me stammer and stut-ter. I flashed back to the hundreds of times she'd said, *"I hope you don't embarrass me again,"* right before introducing me to somebody new, practically guaran-teeing that I'd stumble on the simple words, "Nice to meet you." The memories made my tongue even more uncooperative now, as I faced Nick. It was worse than the day at the restaurant. I wanted to say, "My mother called." Given our previous conversation, that would be enough for him to understand, but I couldn't get past the first *m*. "M-m-m-m—"

"Shhh," Nick said. Not the way my mother had always said it. Not meaning "Be quiet until you can talk right." Not meaning "Quit making a fool of yourself." This was a sound of comfort. Of compassion. It was a sound that meant, "I understand."

And then he stepped forward and pulled me into his arms.

Relief swept through me like a drug in my veins. It made me limp, and I clung to him. I breathed in his smell, part disinfectant, part soap, a hint of the animals he worked and lived with every day. I let the comfort of his apartment and his presence wash over me. My heart slowed. The anger and resentment my mother had stirred in me faded into the background.

"What happened?" he asked.

"My m-m-mother called. They're coming to visit in December."

"Oh, hon. I'm sorry. I'm so sorry she upsets you like this."

"I'm fine." And I was. Standing there in his arms, I felt good. I relaxed against him, and he continued to hold me. He ran his hands up and down my back. He rocked me a little, almost as if we were dancing. I felt at peace. I felt whole and healthy and right. I felt....

Well, I was beginning to feel more than a little aroused, and if the growing bulge against my hip was any indication, I wasn't the only one.

This was what I wanted. Not just Nick, with his strong arms and gentle hands. Not just the comfort of

being with him, but the feeling of normalcy that came
with desire and with feeling desired.

I pulled away enough to meet his eyes. "Will you
kiss me?"

He smiled, a sad, sweet smile. He put his hand behind my neck and pulled me close again. He did kiss
me, but not as I'd hoped. Not on the lips. He kissed my
cheek, and the sensitive spot in front of my ear. "You
have no idea how much I'd like to."

"But you won't."

"I'm afraid if I open that door, I'll never be able to
close it again."

"I don't understand."

"I know."

He brushed his lips over my neck, and I tipped my
head back so he could do it more. He sighed, almost a
moan. "You're the sweetest thing I've ever tasted, but if
I did what you want—what *I* want—you'd hate me for
it. I know you don't believe that, but it's true."

I was disappointed, but not terribly. Yes, I wanted
him, but what mattered to me most was being with him.
Feeling like I could be myself.

"Want to watch the rest of the game with me?" he
asked.

"Sure." We settled on the couch together, and he
let me snuggle up next to him, curled into his warmth.
"Will you hold me a bit more?"

"You bet," he said, putting his arms around me.
"That I can do."

Chapter Six

"Do you have any plans for Halloween?"

It was October 29, and I was sitting next to Nick on his couch, eating the blandest popcorn I'd ever tasted. No salt. No butter. It was like eating packing peanuts. "No. And if this has anything to do with June's conjoined twins idea, the answer is 'hell no.'"

He laughed. "Nothing like that, I promise. I wondered if you'd like to come to my office with me and help hand out candy?"

"You're open on Halloween night?"

"Not really. The Light District does this safe Halloween event every year where the kids trick-or-treat at the businesses. I thought it might be fun to have some company."

I didn't have anything better to do, so two nights later, I climbed into the passenger seat of Nick's Tahoe and rode downtown to his veterinary clinic, which sat right on the edge of the Light District. Down the street,

I could see a strangely luminescent glow from behind the buildings.

"Wow. Is that the lights?"

"Yeah. Haven't you been down here?"

"Not often. Not ever for a holiday."

"We'll check it out later." Nick unlocked the door to his office and I followed him inside. I'd expected the waiting room to be as bland and sterile as most doctors' offices. In some ways, it was. The walls were covered with the usual posters detailing healthy diet and weight for both dogs and cats, but they were hard to see through the dozens of paper witches and ghosts that hung from the ceiling.

"Paul's been busy," Nick said, turning on the light. Instead of the normal white incandescence, we were suddenly bathed in orange. The countertop was covered with cotton cobwebs.

Somewhere in the back, a dog began to bark. "I have a few of them here overnight. Give me a minute to check on them and calm that one down."

As soon as he was gone, the door opened and a horde of kids came in. A princess, a Jedi Knight, and a toddling ladybug whose costume was as wide as it was tall. She could barely walk on her own. "Trick or treat!" Through the door, I could see two women standing by the curb, waiting for them.

The kids all stared at me, bags held out in front of them. I searched behind the counter and came up with a bowl of SweeTarts. I tucked it under my arm and began handing out candy with my right hand.

"What happened to your arm?" the princess asked.

The Jedi elbowed her. "Don't be rude."

I blushed. My tongue turned heavy. I didn't dare speak. I was relieved when they went back out the door.

"Wow, they're starting early this year," Nick said, emerging from the back. He'd changed clothes. He still wore jeans, but now he sported a baggy striped convict shirt and a black mask over his eyes.

"Nice costume."

"Don't laugh. I have one for you too."

It was a T-shirt with the Superman logo, a red mask, and a cape. "Are you serious?"

"Be glad I didn't buy you the blue spandex pants." He looked pointedly toward my groin and winked at me. "Kind of regretting that decision now, to be honest."

My cheeks began to burn, but it was a pleasant kind of embarrassment. I went into the bathroom to change so he wouldn't see me fumbling with my shirt. It wasn't lost on me that he'd given me the superhero costume. When I emerged, the bowl of SweeTarts had been replaced by a bowl full of Halloween pencils, tops, whistles, and glow sticks. "I think they'd rather have the candy," I said to Nick.

"I refuse to hand that shit out. It's not good for them." In the back of the building, the dog began to bark again. This time a second dog joined her. He sighed. "Listen, do you mind handling things on your own for a bit? This will go better if I take them on a quick walk."

"Sure." I sounded more confident than I felt. I hoped every group of kids didn't ask about my arm, but it was only five minutes later when the subject came up again.

"What happened?" a Power Ranger asked me.

I faltered, not knowing what to say, until June popped into my mind. "It was ea-eaten by a bear," I stuttered.

His eyes went wide. "Wow! That's awesome!"

I couldn't help but smile, pleased with my response. "No kidding."

After that I quit worrying about it so much.

Nick wandered in and out, sometimes helping, but he seemed to be inclined to spend most of his time in the back with the animals entrusted to his care.

"Are they all sick?" I asked.

"No, not really. Most of the ones here tonight are from the humane society. I do their spays and neuters for free." He shrugged. "But right now they mostly want attention."

Which was why he was in the back when I had my first childless visitor. He wore a ruffled shirt, a pirate hat, and a plastic hook on his right hand. "Hey!" he said. "You must be Owen. I've heard all about you. I'm Paul. I work for Nick."

He stuck his right hand out, then laughed when he realized it was still covered with the plastic hook. He reached to take it off, and as he did, his eyes landed on my truncated left arm.

The smile fell from his face in a second flat. He went pale. "Oh God," he said, looking pointedly back at my face. "Umm… wow. I'm sorry?"

It was said like a question, as if he wasn't sure whether I wanted to be apologized to or not. I wasn't sure either. "I guess Nick didn't actually tell you *all* about me, did he?" I asked, trying for a lighthearted tone.

"I'm really sorry."

"For what? Wearing a Halloween costume?"

He laughed nervously. "This might be the most awkward thing I've ever done."

Which was exactly why I'd become something of a hermit. That kind of thing happened to me all too often.

"Where's Nick?" Paul asked.

"In the back."

"Oh. Good." His smile turned mischievous. He leaned closer and lowered his voice. "So, tell me. Are you Nick's boyfriend?"

The directness of the question embarrassed me. "No."

Paul was clearly disappointed by my answer. "Are you sure?"

I thought about what had happened the week before. About how it had felt to have Nick's hand cupping my groin. "I think I'd know if I was." But my voice came out shaky.

"So is he gay?"

I wasn't sure how to answer. I was pretty sure he was, but it seemed strange to have Paul ask me. "You've known him longer than I have."

"Yeah, but he's really elusive about the whole thing, you know? I always thought he was straight, but after we helped him move, El said he was pretty sure I had that wrong." He shrugged. "I don't know. Maybe he's just not out?"

Was Nick in the closet? That might explain his sudden about-face after making a move on me, but somehow it didn't fit. He was too confident to be in denial about his sexuality. "I don't think that's it."

"But you *do* think he's gay?"

I felt my cheeks begin to turn red. "Pretty sure, yeah."

He grinned at me. "So you *are* his boyfriend!"

I was saved from answering by a swarm of trick-or-treaters. I'd never been so relieved to see packs of children in my life. Butterflies, fairies, stormtroopers, several things I couldn't identify.

"What happened to your arm?" one of them asked.

"Bear attack," I said, more confident this time.

By the time they were gone, Nick was back. "Since you're here," he said to Paul, "will you cover for a bit so we can go look around?"

"Only if I get to hand out actual candy."

"What's wrong with the stuff I bought?"

Paul laughed. "Halloween isn't about pencils! It's about treats! They don't say 'trick or school supplies,' do they?"

Nick made a low, angry noise that sounded suspiciously like a growl. "I hate what they've done to Halloween. I refuse to buy into the idea that getting factory-wrapped candy bars is somehow better for our kids than getting apples from their neighbors."

"Don't tell me you actually liked getting apples on Halloween," I said. Although if anyone did, it would be Mr. Healthy Diet.

"Besides, you're not handing out apples either," Paul pointed out.

"My point is, the whole 'razor blade in the apple' thing is nothing but an urban legend. Yet we've let ourselves be convinced that things like homemade popcorn balls are dangerous, whereas store-bought candy is good."

I thought about Nick's popcorn. I couldn't blame a kid for wanting candy instead.

Paul shook his head in amusement. "You should hang out with El. He's been raving for weeks about how Halloween has been ruined."

"He's right."

Paul rolled his eyes in my direction, smiling as if we shared a secret. Nick didn't see it because he was rooting around in a cabinet.

"We'll be back in half an hour or so." He pulled out Paul's bowl of SweeTarts and shoved them into his chest. "Happy now?"

Paul grinned at him. "Ecstatic."

I OPTED to leave the mask and cape behind, although I kept the T-shirt on. I put on my jacket and Nick and I waded through fallen leaves and costumed kids toward the heart of the Light District.

Nick pushed his mask up onto his head in order to glance sideways at me. "Let me guess. Paul was giving you the third degree."

"He wanted to know if you're gay."

He laughed, shaking his head "He's kind of clueless, but he's a good guy. Great at his job too."

"Well, you are, right?"

"Great at my job?"

"No. Gay."

He looked over at me with obvious amusement. "I thought I'd been pretty damn obvious about it. With you, at least."

"But why doesn't Paul know? You don't seem like the closeted type."

"Partly, I'm a private person. I never felt the need to advertise it. But partly, I have to admit, I just like to keep Paul guessing."

We rounded the corner, and I stopped in my tracks. Tonight the Light District truly lived up to its name. Hundreds of strands of lights hung from the trees—white, orange, and yellow, reminding me of iridescent candy corn. Some of the trees still had leaves. Others were bare. Glowing ghosts swayed in the branches. Up and down the sidewalk, at least a dozen different inflatable decorations stood guard in front of businesses.

Packs of children ran laughing, bags held tight in their hands. Parents strolled behind, checking their watches, waving to one another.

"It's beautiful," I said.

"Yeah, it is a nice night," Nick said, clearly missing my point. "I'm glad we have good weather for once. Seems like Halloween in Colorado is cold more often than not, and it's never fun to have to put a coat on over your costume."

"Did you grow up here?"

"In Grand Junction. How about you?"

"Laramie. Halloweens there were always windy as hell."

"I thought every day in Wyoming was windy as hell."

"Good point."

I followed him through the plaza, gazing around like an awestruck kid. I was amazed not just at the lights, but at the entire atmosphere of the place. There was so much laughter. The district felt festive and cozy at the same time. I began to notice how many same-sex couples held hands. How many children were escorted by two moms or two dads. The ice cream shop was practically bubbling with energy and laughter. Kids giggled over cups of ice cream crawling with candy worms.

I moved closer to Nick, and he put his arm over my shoulders. I heard Paul's voice in my head. *So you are his boyfriend!* At that moment, it almost felt true, but I didn't dare assume anything.

"Here," Nick said, stopping in front of a door that said Ink Springs. "Come in and meet Seth."

The bell on the door jingled as it closed behind us, and Nick pulled his arm away from me. A bearded man

with more ink than skin scowled at us, and I felt Nick
go stiff beside me. "Seth here?"

He didn't get much more than a grunt in return, but
the man ducked into the back, and a second later Seth
appeared. "This is a nice surprise," he said to Nick.
"You here to do more work on that shoulder?"

"No. I wanted to introduce you to Owen. He lives
above me."

Seth turned an appraising eye my way, looking me
up and down without embarrassment. I began to blush
when his gaze reached my arm, but Nick said, "He's
trying to figure out if you have any ink."

Seth laughed. "He knows me too well. Always trying to scope out people's art."

"No tattoos," I said.

Seth's smile grew exponentially. "Nice going,
Nick! You brought me a blank canvas to work on." He
looked again at my arm. "Good skin too. Not much hair
to worry about." He took a binder off the counter and
handed it to me. "Pick something. My chair's empty
tonight. I'll give you the Virgin Discount."

For half a second I wondered how he knew I was
a virgin. Then I realized he wasn't talking about my
sexual status but about my lack of tattoos.

They were both watching me, expecting a reaction.
The binder was big, so I put it on the countertop in order to avoid having to balance it on my stump while I
looked, and opened it. The first page was full of snakes
and scorpions. Nick laughed. "I don't think those are
your style."

"I don't have a style."

"Not yet," Seth said, rubbing his hands together
with excitement. "That's what's so great about your

first time. It's like setting the mood, you know? Priming the wick. Popping your cherry."

I wondered if it was intentional that he kept using sexual references. I flipped to another page and found flowers and butterflies. Another page held tribal bands.

"You've seen Nick's ink, right?" Seth asked. "You could do something to match." He winked at Nick. "That'd be cute, doing the couple thing. Matching hearts on your ass or something."

My cheeks began to burn. My hand shook as I turned the page. I didn't dare look up.

Nick laughed without embarrassment. He flipped the book closed and pushed it across the counter toward Seth. "Not tonight."

"Too bad." Seth smiled at me. "The offer stands, though. Anytime."

"Thanks," I said, although I had no intention of taking him up on it.

Nick held the door for me. He didn't seem to mind that everybody thought we were a couple. It made me feel reckless and brave, ready to reach out and take his hand, but then I remembered the way he'd pulled away. I was still thinking about it when he put his arm over my shoulder again, drawing me into his warmth.

I decided to stop worrying about what I meant to him and just enjoy it, whatever it was. I leaned into him, feeling more content than I had in ages.

We were ten yards away when the door to Ink Springs opened and Seth called after us, "I see that, Nick! Double discount if you do the hearts!"

By THE time we made it back to the clinic, my smile felt like a permanent part of my face. Paul had handed out all of his candy and was back to distributing Nick's pencils.

"This trick-or-treat thing only goes another hour," he said to us before he left. "You should come down to Tucker Pawn afterward. A few of the guys are stopping by."

It wasn't until he was locking the front door of his clinic that Nick asked, "Do you want to go? I know you're not crazy about that kind of thing."

I didn't want to. Not really. I pictured a raging party, plastic cups full of beer, people playing drinking games. And me standing alone on the outskirts. But I also felt like he wanted me to say yes, and I wanted him to be pleased with me.

"Maybe."

He smiled. "I'll make you a deal. We'll drop by and say hello, but the minute you want to leave, we will. I promise."

As soon as we walked into the back room of Tucker Pawn, I realized how ridiculous my assumptions had been. This wasn't college and these weren't frat boys. They were adult men, not doing keg stands or acting stupid, but just hanging out and talking, sitting on a sagging couch and a few teetering barstools. They laughed a lot, but this gathering was more about stealing an hour or two of adult camaraderie than getting shit-faced.

Nick introduced me around the room. First to Paul, who I already knew, and his partner, El, who owned the pawnshop. Then El's friend Denver—whom I immediately recognized as The Hero from Regina's moving crew—and his boyfriend, Adam, who seemed almost as shy as me. The third couple in the room were Jason, who apparently owned a nightclub that wasn't open yet, it being so early in the evening, and his partner, Michael. One single man, Nathan, rounded out the group.

I took off my jacket and did my best not to be self-conscious about my bare amputated arm hanging from my Superman sleeve. I looked around, trying to figure out if I could ever fit in with this group. Denver and El made more noise than anybody, and I stayed away from them rather than risk attracting their attention, not because they seemed mean but because I knew I'd never be able to keep up with their conversation. I found an empty stool and perched on it.

"We can leave right now if you want," Nick said to me.

"I'm fine." I wasn't sure if it was true. Nick left to find the bathroom and I sat there by myself, feeling nervous and ignored, until Adam brought me a drink.

"I'm not really the partying type either," he said quietly.

I laughed, more out of nervous energy than actual humor. "Is it that obvious?"

He smiled. "Like recognizes like, you know what I mean?" He looked around the room. "Sometimes they still make me nervous too, but they're all nice, I swear."

Only a few words, but I did feel better knowing I wasn't the only introvert in the room. I began to relax by degrees. It didn't hurt that Jason and Adam kept handing me shots. Michael, Paul, and Nick began discussing the plausibility of veterinary acupuncture, and I found myself suddenly sitting with Nathan.

He was young and cute, in a twink kind of way. I had to wonder if he was more than nineteen, although given the fact that Jason was getting him drunk too, I assumed he was at least twenty-one. His hair was blond with pink highlights, and he pulled his own stool close enough that I could make out green eyes behind his hipster frames.

"So what's your part in this little group? Do you work for Jason?" I asked.

"No. I'm Michael's receptionist. He has an acupuncture clinic down the street." He nodded toward Nick. "And you. You're the man who finally landed Hacktown's most eligible bachelor?"

"N-n-no. We're friends. That's all."

He didn't even blink at my stutter, but his eyes widened in pleasant surprise. "Really?" He moved closer. His eyes sparkled mischievously. "So that means you're single?"

"I guess."

He laughed. "Then I should get you another drink."

"No, thanks. I think I've had too many already."

He looked down at my left arm and frowned a bit. I knew the look. He wasn't disturbed so much as unsure if he was allowed to mention it or not.

I thought about what Nick had said to me over sandwiches at the Vibe. *Most people are trying to treat you the way they think you want to be treated.* The bear attack story seemed like the wrong tack here. Instead I took a deep breath and said, "Amniotic band syndrome. I was born without it."

He smiled, obviously relieved I'd brought it up. He reached out and put his hand on my arm. My breath caught in my throat. A lifetime of hiding it, and this was twice in one month that somebody I barely knew had touched it, not with distaste, but with tenderness. I found myself melting into his touch.

He leaned close. "Can I ask you a rude question?"

"I guess."

"Have you ever, you know, used it on somebody? I mean, I know guys who'd love that. Like fisting, but without the fist."

It took a bit of effort not to gape in astonishment. I had no idea what to say. What he was suggesting had never occurred to me. I was also surprised by his assumption that I had any kind of sexual experience, let alone something so kinky. It was kind of nice to know I didn't have Twenty-Eight-Year-Old Virgin oozing from my pores. "Are you serious?"

He laughed. "Yeah. Don't tell me you're one of those prudes who never watches porn?"

I wasn't that sheltered or naïve, but still, I'd never seen anything like what he was referring to. "Everybody I've ever seen in porn has all four limbs intact."

"I think you mean 'all five limbs.'"

Now it was my turn to laugh. I was surprised at how easily the laughter came to me. At how quickly my discomfort with him had fallen away. "Good point."

He let go of my arm to make a dismissive gesture with his hand. "Don't worry. I won't ask you to do it to me. That's not my thing." This time he put his hand on my thigh. He leaned even closer. I wondered if he was about to kiss me. "Are you sure I can't bring you another drink? Or we could go someplace else?"

The possibilities loomed in front of me. I could have this boy take me home, and I'd no longer be a virgin. That was absolutely clear. I wasn't sure how I felt about that. He was cute, and the idea of kissing him certainly appealed. I thought about being skin to skin under the covers, and there was no denying the way it made my pulse race. But when I pictured being kissed, or making love, or waking up next to somebody in the morning, it wasn't Nathan I saw in my head.

It was Nick.

I looked around for him and found him watching me with obvious disapproval. I was also pretty sure he was at least a little bit jealous.

I stopped Nathan's hand on my leg. "I think I'm not as single as I led you to believe."

He laughed, not with annoyance or disdain but with genuine understanding. He backed up, letting the space between us become more casual than intimate. "No harm, no foul, right? I didn't offend you?"

"Not at all."

In fact, I felt sexy. Flattered. Almost invincible. I also knew now exactly what I wanted. When Nick walked over and said, "Let's get you home," I gladly complied.

The cool night air of the Light District surprised me. I tried to remember how many shots I'd had. Enough to make me happily tipsy and uncharacteristically bold. "Coming to my rescue?" I asked Nick as we made our way back to his Tahoe.

His laugh was a sharp and loud. "I wanted to rip his arm off for touching you."

Was it horrible that his jealousy made me feel like I could fly? "Then there'd be two one-armed men for you to deal with."

He laughed, more genuinely this time. "Bad choice of words. Sorry about that."

"I don't mind."

I looked down at the Superman T-shirt I still wore. I really did feel bulletproof.

I reached out with my right hand and smiled like a fool when Nick took it.

Chapter Seven

NICK DIDN'T leave me at my door. He followed me inside, kicked off his shoes, and sat down on my couch. I sat next to him, my heart racing with the possibilities.

"You going to take Seth up on his offer?"

"You mean getting a heart tattooed on my ass?"

He laughed. "Well, I wasn't thinking that exactly."

"Unlikely." I thought about Seth asking me if I'd seen Nick's tattoos. I hadn't, and suddenly I wanted to. More than anything. The alcohol, Nathan's flirting, Nick's attentions—all of it combined to give me courage I wouldn't normally have. I turned to him, straddling his lap. "I never have seen your ink."

"You can see it without sitting on my lap."

"What fun would that be?"

"Owen, this is a bad idea."

"So what? You eat bland popcorn. You don't drink. You don't even believe in Halloween candy." I slid my hand under his shirt, up his smooth stomach. He sucked in his breath, and his eyes drifted shut. I leaned forward and kissed his jaw. "Do something dangerous. Let me see."

"No. I really should leave."

He didn't leave, though, and when I began to tug on his shirt, he helped me pull it up, over his head. He moaned when I put my hand on his bare chest.

His tats were mostly black. V-shaped birds rose from his waistband, across his chest, over one shoulder. The opposite shoulder was half-covered with some kind of intricate knot-like pattern, obviously unfinished. I traced the birds with my fingertips, from the top down. As my fingers made their way down his stomach, his hands clenched on my thighs. His breathing quickened.

I leaned close, wondering if I had enough nerve to do more.

"Owen," he said, his voice hoarse and rough. "Jesus, I shouldn't be doing this. I should have let you go home with that kid."

"I didn't want him. I want you."

"I can't."

"Yes, you can."

"I've spent the last five years making sure I didn't end up in situations like this, but four weeks with you and every ounce of restraint I've ever had is gone."

"I don't want you to have restraint." I put my right arm around his neck. I put my forehead against his. "I want you to kiss me."

He groaned, and I knew I was close. I knew that whatever reasons he had for denying me were crumbling beneath the weight of our shared desire. I steeled all of my nerve and pressed my lips against his.

It wasn't much of a kiss, both of us frozen there, but I felt his resolve fail. He moaned, and in that one

second, our lips touching and my heart thundering in
my ears, he surrendered. He went soft against me and
opened his mouth. His tongue teased my lips, asking
for entrance, and I granted it. I parted my lips and let
him in.

It felt like being claimed. I could have come right
then. The sheer joy of it, his tongue invading my mouth,
the taste of him and the weight of his strong body as he
shifted our positions, bearing down on me. He pushed
me back onto the couch, straddling my hips, pinning
me beneath him. He kissed me harder, sucking at my
upper lip, but when I slid my hand down his stomach,
toward the buttons on his jeans, he stopped me. He
grabbed my wrist and pinned it to the couch at my side.

"My way," he said, his voice thick with arousal. "I
call the shots here. No questions. No arguing."

I didn't know exactly what he meant by that, but
looking into his eyes, I saw no room for argument. I
had no idea what I was about to agree to—if he'd pull
out a leather hood or order me to my knees—but at that
moment, I didn't care. "Anything."

He smiled, and although he still held my wrist, his
grip became a caress. He leaned down to brush his lips
across mine. "You have no idea how many times I've
thought about doing this."

I could only whimper as he kissed me again, not
with the urgency of before, but with a gentleness that
surprised me. He began to explore me, running his
hands up and down my body, moaning against my lips
as I arched into his touch. It was the most sensuous
torture imaginable, the way his hands moved, never
undressing me, but teasing over my stomach, my nipples, down my arms, yet rarely touching my bare flesh.

Never moving to the parts of me that longed most for his attention.

"Let me touch you," I begged. He was still straddling me, and I could feel his erection through his jeans. "Please."

He sat up suddenly, and I worried that I'd angered him—that he was going to stop—but instead, he smiled at me. It was the sexiest, most flirtatious smile I'd ever seen on his face. "I think we can do better than the couch, don't you?"

I didn't care where we were. The couch, the floor. Anywhere was fine with me, so I didn't object when he took my hand and led me to the bedroom. He undressed me quickly, pulling at my clothes until I stood naked and self-conscious before him, my erection sticking out in front of me.

"You're perfect," he said, kissing me, running his strong hands up my back. "I could lick you all over."

I laughed shakily, unbelievably aroused by the idea. He slid his hand down my spine. His fingers caressed between my cheeks. I tensed a bit despite myself, and when he applied pressure to my rim, I gasped.

He moaned into my ear. He turned me around and pushed me gently facedown on the bed. He gripped my cheeks, pulling them apart. I was suddenly tense and terrified. I'd never done this before. Should I tell him? It seemed like I should, but I was too afraid.

"I'm not going to fuck you," he said. "Try to relax."

That was good to know, but I was still nervous. "I don't know if I can."

He kissed his way down my spine, making me shiver. When he reached the top of my ass crack, he spread my cheeks wide. I felt exposed, and far more vulnerable than I'd anticipated. I instinctively flinched away.

Nick let me go. He moved up, his weight comfortable and warm on my back. "Owen," he whispered in my ear. "Have you ever bottomed before?"

I shook my head.

He held very still for a moment. I wished I could see his expression. Then he asked the question I was dreading. "Have you ever topped before?"

I shook my head again.

"Oh Jesus," he moaned in dismay, putting his head down on my shoulder. "I'm such an ass. I shouldn't be doing this."

"No! Don't you dare stop now!"

His laugh was shaky, but he kissed the back of my neck. "We can't have sex anyway. Not like that." He put his fingers between my cheeks again, gently massaging my rim. "No wonder you're so tight."

"I've never really understood how bottoming could feel good."

"It does, though, believe me. It can be the best feeling in the world. I miss it so much. This was my favorite, to be right where you are now, flat on my stomach." He sat up, straddling my thighs. He was still wearing his jeans, but he rocked against my ass as if thrusting into me, causing exquisite friction between my cock and the bed. "Just like this," he said. "I'd trade places with you in an instant if I could."

I had to clear my throat before I could speak. "I wouldn't mind."

He was quiet for a moment, and then he asked in hushed voice, "Do you have any condoms?" He sounded strangely apprehensive about it.

"We just established that I'm a virgin, remember?"

He laughed, and I wondered if it was my imagination that he sounded relieved. "Well, then, looks like neither one of us will be bottoming tonight." He leaned down again to kiss the back of my neck. "No problem. There are plenty of other ways for me to get you off." He moved his hand down my side, around the front of my hip, and I shifted to allow his hand to slide under me. He wrapped his hand around my aching cock, and I moaned, pushing into his fist.

His weight on my back eased a bit. "Turn over."

I did, already breathing hard, anticipating what was to come. His hand was gentle but firm as he stroked me. He kissed my jaw, my neck, my chest. When he reached my nipples, I gasped in surprise, arching into him. I couldn't believe how good it felt, and I gripped his head, pulling him in for more. My hips began to move of their own accord, bucking up and down, thrusting through his hand.

"Nick," I gasped, and he let me go.

"Shhh," he soothed with a smile as he kissed me. "Not yet, baby. Slow down."

"I can't." I'd already waited twenty-eight years. Wasn't that enough?

He chuckled and moved back to my nipples, but this time without stroking my cock. He teased me until each one was wet and red and aching.

Then he moved down.

I gasped again as he pushed my legs apart and my knees up. He put his tongue between my legs, below my scrotum. He began to suck and lick my tender flesh, sometimes moving up to lap at my testes, sometimes moving back down to my perineum. I lay panting and writhing, tugging at his hair until he let me lead him up, up, up, his tongue leaving a hot, wet trail along my

length. When he finally touched my frenulum, I nearly
came. Only the fact that he pulled away for a second
saved me.

"Oh Jesus," I panted.

And in the very next second, he teased his tongue
over that spot again, and when my hips instinctively
rose, he parted his lips and let me slide deep into his
hot, wet mouth.

It was amazing. Scintillating. Utterly exquisite. He
moaned, and I felt the vibrations in my cock. He swallowed me all the way to my root, until I could feel his
nose against my pubic bone. He let me hold him there
while I marveled at the ecstasy of it. While I reminded
myself to breathe. Then I let him go, and he started to
move. Up and down while I lay helpless beneath him,
overwhelmed by the pleasure of it. It was better than
I'd ever imagined. So much better than masturbation.
It wasn't as simple as the pure sexual pleasure of my
cock in his mouth. It was a joy that went beyond the
physical. A warmth that filled me from the inside out. It
was believing I was normal and knowing I was desired.
It was the newfound hope that my life really could be
more. But more than anything, it was about Nick—his
hands on my hips, his weight on my body, his hair tan-
gled in my hands. It was about trusting him. About feeling safe and cherished and utterly at peace with the man
who had so readily become my hero.

He released my cock and moved up to kiss me,
deep and passionate, and I wrapped my arms around
him, the ruined one and the good one both, and I let him
ravage my mouth. I loved the taste of him. The urgency
of his kiss and the gentleness of his touch. I sighed as
he fingered my nipples. When he reached for my cock,
I moaned, pushing toward his hand. My climax was

close, an ache deep in my abdomen, a glorious pressure in my balls.

"Nick," I whispered, not wanting it to end but also not wanting to lose it at an inopportune moment.

"I know, hon. I've got you." He moved quickly down to roll his tongue around the head of my cock, and when I gripped his head, he took me in, swallowing me deep once again.

My hips bucked. A hoarse cry built in my throat. I thrust into the heat of his mouth. Once. Twice. And then I was climaxing, pumping into him, feeling as if he was pulling it out of me. I spasmed again and again, emptying myself, and still he held me, sucking me, moaning as he swallowed my seed.

I'm no longer a virgin.

Others might have quibbled over the correctness of that statement since it had only been oral sex, but I wouldn't have listened. I laughed with the joy of it. I *wasn't* a virgin. Not like I had been. And most importantly, Nick had been my first.

He suddenly loomed above me, smiling. "What's so funny?"

"Nothing. Oh my God, Nick." I pulled him down and kissed him again. "That was…." I floundered for a word that could actually capture how amazing I felt.

"Fun?"

I laughed. "That's a bit of understatement, but yeah."

He smiled and kissed the tip of my nose, then flopped down on the bed next to me, staring up at the ceiling, his hand resting on my hip. He sighed happily.

"What about you?"

His laugh was sheepish. "I'm good," he said with obvious embarrassment, "although I made a hell of a mess in my pants."

I feared my smile would split my face in two. I'd been worried that he hadn't enjoyed it as much as I had, that he was doing it as some kind of favor, but now I knew the truth. The idea of him coming while he sucked me made me giddy.

"There are clean boxers in the top drawer." I felt silly as soon as I said it. It wasn't like he had far to go to get his own pants. "Unless you'd rather go home."

"I think I will go downstairs to change, but I'll come back. If that's okay with you."

My smiled managed to grow even bigger. "I'd like that."

"Can I bring the dogs?"

"Of course."

I climbed under the covers. The alcohol made me sleepy. Slaked lust made me feel heavy and boneless. I quickly fell asleep, rousing only a bit when Nick came back in with the dogs. I heard them sniffing around the room. Nick climbed under the covers with me.

I moved over, seeking the warmth of his body. He put his arm around me, but he was stiffer than I expected.

"We need to talk," he said.

"Tomorrow," I mumbled, and plummeted back into the abyss.

I WOKE feeling like I'd been zipped into a mummy-style sleeping bag designed for a ten-year-old. It took me a second to figure out why I couldn't move. Bert lay on top of the blankets on one side of my legs, and Bonny on the other, pinning me in. On the other side of the bed, Betty lay stretched across the pillow. I didn't see Nick.

"They're not supposed to sleep on the bed," Nick said from behind me. "But they do it anyway."

I turned to find him sitting in the chair in the corner of the room. Normally it was the catchall for my laundry, but he'd pushed the stack of clothing to the floor. It was dark enough in the room to hide his expression from me, but not to obscure the fact that he was fully dressed.

"Sneaking away in the night?" I meant it as a joke, but he didn't laugh.

"Owen, we need to talk."

The weight of his words and the solemn timbre of his voice scared me. My chest felt heavy with dread. "No."

"Yes."

I sat up, suddenly unable to bear being pinned in by the dogs. I pulled my legs free of the covers and stood up. I felt vulnerable being naked in front of him when he was dressed, so I pulled a pair of boxers out of my drawer and donned them before turning to face him across the dark room. "I don't want to talk because I know what you're going to say."

"And what is that?"

"That it shouldn't have happened. That it can't happen again."

He didn't answer, but his silence was more damning than any words.

"I'm right, aren't I?"

"It was a mistake."

"No! Goddammit, it was *not* a mistake!"

He sighed. "You don't understand."

"You're right, I don't. One minute you're pulling me close, and the next you're pushing me away. You tell me you want me, but as soon as I respond, you say I can't have you. What am I supposed to think?"

"You have every right to be mad, Owen. And confused. And I'm sorry. I'm sorry I let things get out of hand."

"Well, I'm not!" I was embarrassingly close to tears and I fought them back. "I'm *not* sorry!"

"Owen—"

"Is it me?"

"What?"

"Is it me? Am I the problem?"

"No." No hesitation. He said the word with a quiet emphasis that made it difficult to doubt him, and yet I had no other explanation.

"You say you're attracted to me, but the truth is, you can't stand the idea of being with a cripple."

"That's not it."

"You want to touch me, but you hate it when I touch you."

His laugh was harsh and bitter. "Is that really what you think?"

"What other explanation is there?"

He leaned forward and put his head in his hands. "It's not that I don't want you to touch me, Owen. It's that if I let you touch me, I'll lose control, even more than I did tonight."

"Good!"

"It's not good—"

"I want you to lose control like that more often."

"You have no idea what's going on here. You have no idea how dangerous this is."

"Dangerous?"

"I'm trying to protect you."

"From what?"

"From me."

"What the hell is that supposed to mean?" I asked, my anguish suddenly giving way to rage. "Jesus Christ, stop speaking in riddles and talk to me!"

"Owen—"

"You're not making any sense at all!"

"Listen to me—"

"You're making excuses!"

"I'm HIV-positive."

It was the last thing I'd expected to hear. All the air seemed to be sucked from my lungs. It was like being punched in the stomach.

I backed up until I hit the wall, overwhelmed and horrified. The room seemed to shrink, becoming too small to hold us both. I wished I was somewhere else. *Anywhere* else. I wanted put miles between us. To be far, far away rather than face the possibility of this disease. My legs could no longer hold me. I fell heavily to the ground. All I could think of was my cock in his mouth. The virus possibly moving through my body already, attacking my cells, destroying my ability to fight infections. My stomach roiled, the alcohol turning sour. My hands shook.

Was Nick going to die?

Was I?

My head began to spin. My breathing took on a life of its own. I wondered wildly if this was what it felt like to hyperventilate. I leaned forward, bracing myself on the floor, trying not to be sick in front of him. "But tonight, we…. Oh God."

"Nothing we did puts you at risk," he said quietly. "I would never do that to you."

"But we had sex!"

"Owen, I was careful about exactly what activities we engaged in. Saliva is a very poor carrier of the virus. You don't have any open wounds. And my viral load is low right now. I was mindful of the possibilities. I promise you, what we did tonight is as close to zero-risk as it gets. Me going down on you is about as safe as kissing."

Was that true? I had no idea. I only knew the most publicized facts: it couldn't be passed through casual contact. Even sharing a toothbrush would be safe. But beyond that, I was woefully uneducated. I had to trust that he was telling me the truth.

I closed my eyes and took deep breaths, trying to assess the last few moments. Could this really be happening? His late-night confession in the dark seemed surreal after our magical evening in the colorful lights of downtown, but no matter how much I wanted it to be a nightmare, it wasn't. This was reality.

"How long have you known?"

"Five years."

Five years. The horror began to recede. In its place, I found anger.

"You should have told me."

"I know."

"You should have told me before I let you—" I gestured helplessly toward the bed. "Before we did *that*!"

"You're right. I should have." He put his elbows on his knees and stared at the floor. "In some states, you could press charges against me. I wouldn't blame you if you did. I wouldn't even fight them."

Press charges? Jesus, was that really the way I wanted this to go?

I took a deep breath. And another. My thoughts became less scattered. The real world began to return to its proper place around me. I was crouched on the floor, shivering in my boxers.

He could have kept lying. He could have taken advantage of me in far worse ways. Still, I felt betrayed. I couldn't even think. Not with him there, watching me, waiting for me to react.

I sat back against the wall, hugging my knees. "I'd like you to leave."

Even in the low light, I saw the way he slumped at my words. "Owen—"

"Please."

For a moment he didn't move, and I thought he might argue, but then he sighed instead. He slowly pushed himself up out of the chair, as if it took every ounce of his strength. The dogs all sat up, watching him, suddenly alert.

"Come on," he said to them.

Only after he was gone did I give in. Only then did I put my head down and cry.

Chapter Eight

THE NEXT day was one of the most miserable of my life. As if what had happened with Nick wasn't bad enough, I was also hungover. My head throbbed. I looked down at the pile of clothes next to bed—jeans and a Superman shirt lying where Nick had dropped them as he'd undressed me—and had to run for the bathroom.

I was angry, not so much at Nick as at the universe in general. At fate. At my own terrible luck. I'd finally found a man whom I adored, who liked me, who was attracted to me, who made me feel better than I'd ever felt, only to have the rug ripped out from under me.

HIV.

My head filled with horrible images—the famous photo of David Kirby in the last moments of his life. Only in my mind, it was Nick, his strong, muscular body destroyed by the virus.

How long? I realized I had no idea. The sensationalism of AIDS had long since died. It wasn't that I thought it was gone, or cured, or irrelevant, but somehow I'd never thought much about the fact that it was still out there like some kind of relentless hunter, killing people, ruining lives.

Had he lied about putting me at risk?

I didn't think so. No matter what had happened, I trusted Nick. He could have fucked me. He could have let me fuck him. But he hadn't. He hadn't even taken off his pants. I remembered how he'd seemed relieved when he found out I didn't have condoms. If I had, he might have been tempted to do something riskier, but he'd refrained. *There are plenty of other ways for me to get you off.*

I couldn't decide if the memory was erotic or nauseating. I curled up in my bed, relieved that it was only Saturday. I wouldn't have to face him again until Monday. I spent the day downing Sprite, Advil, and saltine crackers and cursing Jason to the heavens for whatever had been in the shots.

At five o'clock, Nick knocked on my door. I wasn't ready to face him. I wished I could hide, but it was ridiculous. He knew I was home. I pulled on a T-shirt and sweats, ran a hand through my matted hair, and answered the door.

He looked terrible. Probably worse than me. Grief made his face long and haggard. Sorrow clouded his eyes.

"Hey," he said quietly.

I leaned against the doorjamb, unwilling to let him in. Unwilling to admit yet how much he'd hurt me. Or how much I'd hurt him. "Hi."

He slumped a bit, and I almost broke. I almost reached out for him. But my hand was stilled by thoughts of the virus. Before, I'd thought he was perfect. Now, right or wrong, he seemed tainted.

"Owen, I want to tell you how sorry I am. I—"

"I don't want to talk about it." A lump began to form in my throat. I wanted to end this conversation before I started crying again.

He nodded. "Okay. Well, I want you to know...." His voice cracked and he stopped. He pinched the bridge of his nose. He was as close to tears as I was. "I don't expect anything big. I just hope we can be friends again. That's all."

I nodded, unable to speak. Unable to hold my tears at bay. I closed the door, put my head against the wood, and cried.

Partly, I cried for myself.

Mostly, I cried for Nick.

I SPENT the next couple of weeks avoiding him as much as I could. I still went to his house for piano lessons, but he seemed to sense my mood, and he gave me a wide berth. I used the key he'd given me to practice while he was at work, although I felt guilty for doing it.

After the second week, as I followed June out the door after our lesson, she turned to face me on the stairs. "What happened between you and Nick?"

I shrugged, trying to act casual. "Nothing. Why?"

She chewed her lip, watching me with obvious skepticism, weighing her words, trying to decide how much to say. "Did he tell you about being sick?" she finally asked.

I ducked my head. It was getting dark outside, and the light wasn't good on the stairway, but I couldn't hide my discomfort.

"And then what?" She practically spat the words at me. "You suddenly decided you couldn't be friends with him because he has HIV? You think you're too good for him now?"

"No, but I think he should have told me sooner."

"Do you have any idea what his privacy means to him? Have you even considered what it's like for him, being 'that guy with HIV'?"

"Maybe a bit like being 'that guy with one arm.'"

"Yeah, except nobody treats you like you're contagious."

I hung my head again, even more ashamed than before. June sighed, and the anger seemed to drain out of her. "He misses you. I don't know if he'll tell you on his own, so I'm telling you instead. He's miserable. I don't think I've seen him so depressed since he was diagnosed."

I was miserable too. I couldn't help wondering if it would be better to be miserable together.

I LAY in bed that night, thinking about Nick.

Learning about his disease, suddenly realizing that heroes could fall too, had been heartbreaking, but I began to see how selfish my reaction had been. June was right. I shouldn't have abandoned him. We were friends, and that wasn't how friends behaved.

But what about the rest?

I was attracted to Nick. Who wouldn't be? He was fun and confident and sexy. He made me comfortable in a way nobody else could. He flirted with me and made me feel desirable for the first time in my life. But if we were to remain friends, I had to put all that aside.

It was normal for me to desire him. After all, I was twenty-eight, and until Halloween, I'd still been a virgin. I figured anybody in my position would have felt the same. But I realized now what a horrible position I'd put him in. Yes, he was attracted to me, and he cared about me, but he'd tried to keep a few simple boundaries in place, and all the while, I'd pushed him forward, blindly banking on his desire to overcome his will.

It had worked too, but at what cost?

So how would we stay friends, but without the sexual tension? That was the question. And almost as quickly as I thought it, a potential answer came. What if I focused my desire on somebody else? It wasn't that I wanted to hurt Nick or to make him jealous, but maybe if I turned my attentions elsewhere, it would make things easier. It would take the pressure off us both. I couldn't have Nick, but that didn't mean I had to stay single for the rest of my life.

After all, Nick wasn't the only guy who'd flirted with me recently.

It wasn't hard to find Michael's clinic online and get their number. The hard part was picking up the phone and dialing, then staying on the line, waiting for an answer.

"Tucker Springs Acupuncture. This is Nathan. How can I assist you today?"

I'd been counting on him to answer the phone, but for a moment, I wasn't sure what to say. I sat there, frozen and mute.

"Hello-o?" he said. "Does somebody need to be pricked and poked, because you have to speak up if you want me to put you on the schedule."

"Nathan, it's Owen. We met on Halloween. Do you remember me?"

"Owen! How could I forget the man who turned me down cold?"

"Oh. Uh. Yeah. I'm sorry about that."

"No need to apologize. I wasn't exactly interested in having my ass kicked by a studly veterinarian anyway. So, what's up? Do you need an appointment?"

"No. I w-wanted to talk t-to you." I stopped and took a breath, getting my tongue under control. "I wondered if you'd like to meet me for a cup of c-coffee. Or a beer, I guess. Something."

He was silent for a moment, and I started to feel foolish. Why had I called? Why had I assumed one drunken night of flirting meant anything? Then he said, "I get off at five thirty, which means I can be at Mocha Springs Eternal at five thirty-five exactly."

I tried to muffle my sigh of relief. "I'll see you then."

It wasn't until I walked into the coffee shop that I began to regret my decision. First of all, the place was busy. The highly caffeinated after-work crowd swarmed and buzzed around me, and I stepped back outside to wait.

What did I hope to accomplish here? I'd been so nervous, I'd barely managed to eat lunch, and now here I was, my empty stomach rumbling with nerves. What if drinking a double latte made me sick to my stomach? What if it made my stutter worse? What if—

"Owen?"

I turned to find Nathan standing behind me, smiling like a kid. He'd added black tips to his blond and pink spikes. "Hi," I said stupidly.

He gestured into the coffee shop. "Did you want to go in?"

I looked inside, hoping to find a reason to change our plans. "I don't think there are any empty tables."

"Let's get it to go. It's a nice night. We can sit by the fountain."

By the fountain, I realized, meant outside. "Sounds great."

We stood awkwardly next to each other in line, not talking. I managed to order without stuttering too much. It wasn't until we were waiting for our drinks that he said, "I was surprised to hear from you."

"I know it was out of the blue. I hope you don't mind."

"Why would I mind? I could use more calls from cute men."

I laughed, but I was glad when the barista called my name. I followed Nathan outside and into the heart of the plaza. The Light District was beginning to flare to life, although it wasn't dark out yet. "Here," Nathan said, stopping at a bench.

We sat and sipped our coffee, watching the people bustle past us. Parents with their children, friends laughing as they headed for home or an after-work drink, uptight men and women with their cell phones clutched like lifelines to their ears, moving frantically through the crowd. It was Nathan who finally broke the silence.

"Where do you work?"

After that, it got easier. He was good at asking questions and making small talk. He was funny too. He told me about his job and how he was saving his money to buy a horse. But finally he asked the million-dollar question.

"So did you and Nick break up?"

"We weren't really ever together."

"So what was Halloween, then? A one-night stand?"

That was a good question. That certainly wasn't what I'd had in mind. I was pretty sure it wasn't what Nick had wanted either. And yet, what else would it be called?

It made my heart feel heavy in my chest. Was that really what it came down to? I'd lost my virginity, and it was nothing more than a bad cliché? "It's complicated."

Nathan laughed. "Honey, that's the story of my life. You meet somebody. You like them, they like you. Then you get naked together and it all goes to hell."

I couldn't help but laugh. "Wow. I guess it isn't as complicated as I thought."

He put his arm along the back of the bench and rested his hand on my shoulder. He moved closer and leaned toward me, making the public park bench feel intimate. "Is that why you called me? Are you really interested in more complications?"

My stomach fluttered. I was hyperaware of the heat of his hand where it rested on my upper arm. "Maybe." It came out wrong, though. It came out like a question.

He smiled at me and caressed the side of my neck with his fingers. It felt good—soft and sweet—but it made my heart ache. Why had I ever believed I could substitute Nathan for the man I actually cared about?

"Don't get me wrong," Nathan said as if reading my mind. "I'm game if you are. I can be your rebound booty call, if that's really what you want. I don't think it is, though. I think what you really want is him, and when it's all over I don't want you feeling like I took advantage of you."

I ducked my head to hide my blush. "You're way too perceptive."

"One of my better faults." He sat back an inch. He didn't take his hand away from my shoulder, but his touch became less of a caress. It became the solid grip of a friend. "What happened with Nick?"

I shook my head, because I couldn't tell him. I didn't want to betray Nick's secret. But I desperately wanted to talk to somebody. "It's hard to explain. He kept a secret from me, and because I didn't know the truth, I pushed him into something—"

"Sex?"

I nodded. "And then he told me, and everything changed."

"Are you intentionally being vague?"

"Yes."

"You're protecting him?"

Yes, I realized. That was exactly what I was doing. "It's a really personal issue. I understand why he kept it to himself."

"If you were angry, you'd want to get back at him. You'd want to tell me his dirty secret."

"It's not a dirty secret. It's—"

"You just made my point, honey. You're sympathetic, and yet you feel betrayed."

"Exactly."

"And how do you think he feels?"

Alone. And betrayed. Exactly like me.

I was the one who'd pushed for more. I was the one who'd practically begged him to sleep with me. Yes, I could blame him for giving in, but what good would it do me?

"I miss him," I said.

"Then stop missing him. Go throw yourself in his arms. Apologize, or demand an apology, or both. But whatever you do, hang on to him, Owen. Don't let him get away."

Chapter Nine

THE NEXT day I sat down and did the thing I'd been avoiding for over two weeks: I started looking up details on HIV. Now that I'd decided to pull my head out of my ass, I figured I should be thorough.

The first thing I wanted to know was the scariest: How much time did he have? I quickly learned HIV wasn't the death sentence it had once been, especially for healthy individuals undergoing treatment. My research also shed a new light on the way he lived—a healthy lifestyle and a good drug regimen went a long way toward ensuring that a person with HIV could live as long as anybody else. It was entirely possible Nick would survive to be an old man.

I sat back and breathed a sigh of relief for Nick. That was my biggest worry out of the way.

After that I began looking at the data regarding transmission. He hadn't lied to me about putting me at risk. I'd instinctively assumed oral sex involved some

risk, but it wasn't that simple. If I'd been the one sucking him off, the risk would have been slightly higher.
But as long as there were no open wounds, being on
the receiving end of oral sex was absolutely safe. In
fact, a lot of sexual activities could still be enjoyed with
very little risk. Add condoms and a pre-exposure pro-
phylactic drug, and it was entirely possible somebody
who was HIV-negative could stay negative, even if
involved in a sexual relationship with somebody who
was positive.

I wasn't ready to think about that. Not yet.

But I was ready to do what was right.

The next night I had another piano lesson with
June. We were making progress on "Ode to Joy." The
thought of the recital still made me nervous, but I began
to realize that we really might pull this off. June and I
both stayed for a while after Amelia had left, practicing. I was biding my time, waiting for her to leave, and
she seemed to sense my impatience.

"You're not going to be an ass, are you?" she asked
quietly.

"I think I've already been an ass. My plan now is
to *stop* being an ass."

She smiled and kissed me on the cheek. "Good
luck."

Nick had been hiding in the kitchen during our lesson. Ostensibly, he'd been cooking, but it wasn't until
June was leaving that I began to hear the telltale sounds
of pots and pans clanging together. It took every ounce
of nerve I had to walk into his kitchen. He looked up at
me, wary but hopeful, and I froze in my tracks.

"Hi," I blurted out. A stupid, inadequate greeting,
but it was all I had.

"Hi." He glanced down at my chest and smiled. "Nice shirt."

I'd intentionally worn the Superman shirt he'd given me on Halloween, hoping it would help ease the tension between us. It seemed to be working for him, but not so well for me. I hugged my ruined arm against my stomach, took a deep breath, and made myself ask, "Can we talk?"

"Of course." He motioned to a chair. "Have a seat."

I did, and then I sat there watching him, unsure of how to begin. How did you go about asking somebody the details of their HIV status? I thought about how often I'd seen people uncomfortable with me, unable to ask about my arm. I decided Nick's approach was best—direct.

"When we first met, you told me you'd been a shut-in for a while."

"For about a year."

"Because of the HIV?"

He paused briefly in his chopping, then nodded and went on, slowly slicing a carrot into bits. "It was right after I was diagnosed."

"Will you tell me about it?"

He was quiet for a moment, seemingly contemplating where to begin. "I was on vacation with my family, believe it or not. My parents and June and me. We went to Cancun. It was like being a teenager again, you know, going to the beach with my parents and playing in the ocean with my sister. But one night everybody else went to bed early, and I was bored, so I went online and I found a club nearby." He swallowed and set his knife down. His hands were shaking. "And I hooked up with somebody. I took him back to my room. And I spent the next three days with my family, like before, but every night when I got back to my room, he'd be there waiting for me, and we...." He laughed bitterly. "God, we fucked like rabbits, is what we did." He shook his head, looking sightlessly down at the pile of chopped vegetables on the counter. "And the first couple of times, we used condoms, but then we ran out and we just kept going. It was stupid. That's the worst part. I have no excuse whatsoever except I was young and stupid. I was having fun, and I guess I thought it couldn't happen to me, as ridiculous as it sounds." He began scooping the vegetables up and dropping them into a bowl. "I was diagnosed six months later."

"Did he know he was sick?"

"I've wondered, but I have no idea. I never even knew his last name." He leaned forward, closing his eyes, his fingers white-knuckled on the countertop. "Four nights with him, and I've been paying for it ever since." He shook his head. "I can't be that person, Owen. I won't be the one who passes this disease on to somebody else. The only way it ends is if we stop spreading it. What happened between us the other night... God, I can't even tell you how sorry I am for what I did."

"Because you didn't tell me about it first?"

"Yes. And because I should never have let it happen at all."

"I did some research. I know you didn't lie to me about the risks."

"I was careful. But I still feel terrible about it. I can't ever let myself get carried away like that again."

"So, what? Your plan is to never have sex again?"

He laughed, although there wasn't much humor in it. "When you say it that way, it sounds ridiculous."

"Isn't it?"

He jerked into motion as if it pained him, sniffling and wiping at his eyes. I hadn't realized he'd been crying. "Ridiculous or not, it's the only thing that feels right. It's the moral thing to do."

I suspected he was just trying to punish himself more for a few nights of carelessness in his youth, but it didn't seem worth arguing about.

Bert padded across the room to nudge my hand. I scratched his ears and thought about Nick's story so far. "So you caught it in Cancun. What happened after that?"

"Well, I was lucky, in a way, because we caught it early. And because I had insurance, so I could start treatment right away."

"And you kept working?"

"I did, but only because I couldn't afford to lose my coverage. I was like a zombie. I went to work, and I had doctor appointments, and I came home, and that was it. I didn't even spend Christmas with my family that year. All I could do was sit at home and think, 'This is my life. This is it. I'm going to die.'"

"I can imagine it would be easy to give in to depression."

He nodded. "Exactly."

"So what happened?"

"Pink Floyd."

"What?" I asked, laughing despite myself.

He turned to face me for the first time, leaning back against the counter. He didn't look sad anymore. He looked like himself. Like the Nick I'd come to know— confident and in control.

And sexy. No matter what, still sexy.

"I know it sounds stupid, but I was depressed, and I was wallowing in it, and what's better for that than Pink

Floyd, right? I was listening to 'Wish You Were Here.' And there's this line. 'Did you exchange a walk-on part in a war for a lead role in a cage?' And I thought, that's me. That's what I'm doing. I'm living in a cage. And I started to cry." He blushed a bit at that, but he didn't look away. He didn't stop talking. "I started thinking about how much of the world I hadn't seen, and all the things I hadn't done, and I realized that if I never did them, that if I died alone in that apartment, it wouldn't be because of the HIV. It would be because of *me*. Because I was choosing the cage." He reached up to touch his hair, a familiar nervous gesture that made me smile. "So I decided to start over. I moved here and opened my clinic." He crossed his arms and sighed, looking sheepishly down at the floor, suddenly seeming unsure of himself again.

"I never meant for this to happen, Owen. I hope you know that. I've been so careful. I don't go to clubs. I don't date. I don't flirt. You may laugh at this idea of being celibate, but it always felt right. But with you...." He looked up at me, his eyes full of anguish. "I wish I'd done better. I wish I'd told you from the beginning, but it's not something I tell many people. Seth knows because he does my ink, but otherwise I keep it to myself. I've never even told Paul, and I work with him every day."

I could understand why he wouldn't want his HIV status to be common knowledge. "I suppose there's never a good time to share information like that."

"There really isn't. The problem was, I shouldn't have had to. I shouldn't have ever let it get that far. I shouldn't have flirted with you or touched you. I just—" His words jerked to a halt, and he wiped his eyes again, his gaze locked on the floor at his feet. "Something about you makes me want to help you and protect you and spend time with you. It makes me want to… to….”

“Sleep with me?”

He nodded. “That’s not what I was going to say, but yes. That too. I was attracted to you from the very beginning.”

“But you didn’t want to tell me about being HIV-positive.”

“I kept trying to convince myself I didn’t need to, that I could be your friend and not your lover, but then I couldn’t ever keep my hands off you. All those years of abstaining, and suddenly I was like a horny teenager again. You’re like some kind of drug I can’t get out of my system. I don’t know. I realize it’s a lame excuse to say I couldn’t help myself, but it’s the truth.”

“It’s not so lame,” I said, because ridiculous or not, it made my heart swell to hear him say it. “It’s not all your fault, you know. I pushed you pretty hard.”

“I’m not sure that justifies it.”

“I don’t know.” He opened his mouth to object, but I rushed on before he could. “You told me no, Nick. Not just once, but multiple times. I should have respected that, but I didn’t. I knew you were having a hard time keeping your hands to yourself, and I intentionally used it against you. I pushed and pushed until I got what I wanted.”

“Owen, no. Please—”

“No. Listen to me. I know in your mind, I’m some kind of blameless victim, but that’s not how I see it. I coerced you into doing something you didn’t want to do. I refused to take no for an answer. And I’m sorry for that.”

He shook his head. “Please don’t apologize to me. I don’t deserve that.”

I wasn't sure that was true. "I have something to tell you too." I'd thought about this, and although I couldn't put my finger on exactly why it mattered, I knew that it did. "I've told you about my stutter and my mother. But I didn't tell you about what happened to me in high school."

He leaned back against the counter, watching me. Waiting. Patient, as always.

"I met a boy. He was new to our school. He moved in around the block. It was summer break, and he didn't know anybody else, so we became friends. He was patient, you know. The way you're patient. He l-let me talk. He didn't laugh or get annoyed when I stuttered."

"Why do a sense a 'but' coming on?"

"About the time our junior year started, we began fooling around. It wasn't much because we were scared to death. Just touching each other. Making out a bit."

"And your mom caught you?"

"Worse. We got caught at school. Under the bleachers, as cliché as that sounds. We were kissing. That's all. We still had our clothes on and everything, but this was Wyoming, after all. The teacher who caught us was trying to be cool, but the principal freaked. They called my mom. She was furious. Embarrassing her was b-bad enough, starting gossip all over town. But the fact that it was with another *boy*." Up until that point, my mother's attention had always been domineering, but I'd mostly thought it was for my own good. But knowing I was gay seemed to have been the last straw. "And the boy—Jeremy—he told everybody that *I'd* kissed *him*. That he didn't like me and that he was trying to pull away. I couldn't even defend myself. I couldn't stop stuttering enough to g-g-get my w-words out. Anyway,

up until then, I'd been doing better, but after that, everything f-fell apart."

"What do you mean?"

"The stuttering got worse. The few friends I'd
made abandoned me. Jeremy ended up on the wrestling
team, and he called me a f-f-fag every time he saw me.
He and his friends spray-painted my locker and v-van-
dalized my car. I couldn't even look at anybody. And
the worst part of it was, my m-mom acted like I deserved it all. She told me that's what happens to devi-
ants. That maybe being teased would make me think
twice next time, like maybe the bullies could sh-shame
me into being the kind of son she wanted me to be."

Nick scuffed the toe of his sneaker against the
kitchen floor. "I guess that's what angers me the most
about your mom. I mean, here I am, sick because I did
something stupid, and my parents support me no matter what. My sister moved here from Grand Junction
in case I needed help. But your mom blames you for
things that aren't your fault. Your arm, and your stutter,
and being gay." He shook his head in disgust and finally
looked back up at me. "So what happened?"

"Nothing really. I begged to switch schools, and
my dad wanted to let me, but my mom said no. She said
I had to take responsibility for my actions. That running
away was never the answer."

His gaze was sympathetic but unwavering. "Owen,
why are you telling me this now?"

I shrugged. "It seemed like I should. You've been
honest with me, and it was time for me to be honest
with you."

He laughed, but it was a sad sound. "I don't think
you withholding your darkest high school moment is the
same as me not telling you about being HIV-positive."

"I know. But I don't want there to be any more secrets between us."

"Fair enough. No more secrets." He crossed the room and sat down in order to lean close and look into my eyes. "I really am sorry."

"I know. We both screwed up. We're both sorry. How about if we say we're both forgiven too?"

"Works for me."

I wanted to reach out and touch him. To take his hand. But I couldn't. I was still attracted to him, and yet I still couldn't quite wrap my head around the idea of his illness. I couldn't make it fit with the way he looked, so healthy and strong. I couldn't think of how it felt to kiss him without thinking of the virus too.

Still, I missed him.

I cleared my throat and made myself ask, "Can we be friends again?"

"I never stopped being your friend."

"But I feel like I stopped being yours."

He looked down at the floor, rubbing the back of his neck. When he looked up again, there was a tentative smile on his face. "I was about to make dinner."

"You've spoiled me, you know. I'm actually starting to crave broiled fish, and I can't stand to eat frozen pizza anymore."

"Does that mean you'll stay?"

"I'm not going anywhere."

Chapter Ten

FOR THE most part, things between us returned to normal, although there was undeniably more distance between us than before. He stopped flirting with me completely. I missed it, and yet I wasn't sure it would be wise to initiate anything either. We were friends again, and for the moment that felt like enough. I spent evenings at his house practicing while he made dinner, and afterward we'd walk his dogs. I finally canceled my weekly grocery delivery and started driving to the store when I needed something. It was a small step, but it felt momentous, and I began to realize that people didn't stare at me nearly as often as I'd imagined.

"Would you like me to give you a hand out to your car with these?" the girl who bagged my groceries asked one day before she noticed my arm and turned beet red. She gave me that *look*—the look that meant "Oh shit, I hope I didn't just offend this guy." And for possibly the first time, I was able to laugh at such an innocent blunder from an adult.

"I can always use another hand," I told her.

Her relief was almost palpable, and I thought about what Nick had said to me. *Most people are trying to treat you the way they think you want to be treated.* It had taken me twenty-eight years, but I was starting to learn one of my greatest life lessons: high school wasn't a reflection of real life. People were generally good. People like Nick, and like June. Like their friends from the pawnshop, El and Paul and Seth and Michael and Nathan.

Yes, Nathan, who probably had no idea how much he'd helped me. It suddenly seemed important that I tell him.

"Wow," he said when he answered the phone that afternoon. "Will wonders never cease? I'm getting a second call from the mysterious one-armed man?"

"Not much mystery here, I assure you."

"Honey, don't sell yourself short. You need to learn to work what you've got."

"Well, in the meantime, you interested in meeting for coffee again?"

"I'd love to."

It was cooler and windier than the time before, and the coffee shop was warm and cozy, so we opted to stay inside. We settled on a couch in front of the gas fireplace.

"How's the boyfriend?" he asked as we shed our coats.

"He's not my boyfriend."

"I've heard that before, but then you went home with him."

I laughed. He was teasing, and it felt good. I loved the way he could so quickly put me at ease. "Thanks for meeting me again."

"I'm glad you called, even if it isn't to take me up on that offer of a booty call." He leaned a bit closer, more playful than flirtatious. "That isn't why you called, is it?"

"No."

"Damn." But it was said with mock disappointment.

"I wanted to thank you, actually."

"Thank me?" he asked, looking genuinely confused. "For what?"

"For being my friend that day, even though you barely knew me."

He waved his hand at me. "It was nothing."

"No. It wasn't." I hated that I was beginning to blush, but I made myself say the rest. "It meant a lot to me. It helped. So, thank you."

All of his playfulness fell away in an instant. He reached out and took my hand. Not flirting. Not making a pass. Just acknowledging me. "I was happy to do it."

We stayed there another hour, chatting about work and the weather and my upcoming recital. Two months ago, I'd been alone. Now I had friends. More than one, even. It was hard to believe I'd come so far.

NICK'S PARENTS came for Thanksgiving. Despite my newfound confidence, I was nervous about meeting them. "What did you tell them about me?" I asked Nick on the Tuesday before Thanksgiving as we waited for them to arrive.

He laughed. "Not a damn thing, but you can bet June filled them in."

As it turned out, my fears were ungrounded. His parents were as delightful as him and June. Their father had spent his life working construction, and it showed. He was big and burly and seemed to love football more than life itself. He doted on June. Their mother, Truvy, was everything mine wasn't—happy, loving, and supportive. I had worried that she'd be suspicious or curious about my relationship with Nick, but if she wondered, she never let on. She welcomed me into the family like some kind of long-lost nephew.

We spent Wednesday playing board games, and that night we all went out for dinner. Nick took us to the Greek restaurant where we'd had our disastrous first date. It was still crowded, but it felt far less claustrophobic than before. Maybe it was because June was there, spinning some ridiculous tale of how we'd lost our arms while saving a runaway baby carriage from a speeding train. Maybe it was Nick laughing at his sister's antics. Or maybe it was only because I finally realized that nobody was there to judge me. I barely stuttered as I ordered dinner, and the only thing I broke all night was the plate they gave me for that exact purpose.

It felt like victory.

The next day Nick helped his mother cook Thanksgiving dinner while June and her dad watched football. Betty and Bert sprawled next to them on the couch. Bonny stayed in the kitchen, ready to pounce on any scrap of food that hit the floor. I wandered between both rooms, not quite knowing my place, but feeling comfortable nonetheless. My home had never been so peaceful, or so filled with the simple joy of togetherness. I felt like I'd fallen through the rabbit hole and landed in a Norman Rockwell painting. I hoped I never had to leave it.

I was relieved to find that Thanksgiving was one of Nick's splurge days with regard to food. He seemed happy to let his mom take the lead in the kitchen. He didn't mention sodium or trans fats or glutamates even once. He spent more time dipping his fingers into whatever his mom was working on than actually cooking. She swatted at his hand and scolded him each time, but I could tell she loved every minute of it.

"Owen," Truvy said to me at one point, "come stir this cranberry sauce for me. I don't want it to scorch."

I took the spoon and began to stir the bright red concoction. It had actual cranberries in it, which surprised me. "I had no idea you could get cranberry sauce that didn't come from a can."

"This is so much better," Nick said from behind me. He put one hand on the small of my back as he leaned over the stove to look into the pan. "And my mom makes it better than anybody. You'll never eat that fake stuff again."

"I never ate it to begin with."

His mother was on the other side of the room, spreading jarred pimento cheese into celery sticks. She pointed her knife at him. "Your flattery will get you nowhere," she teased.

He laughed. "We'll see."

He started to reach for the spoon, and Truvy said, "Owen, don't let him have it! If he starts tasting it now, there won't be any left and he'll have a stomachache for the rest of the night."

"I was ten when that happened. I think I've learned my lesson."

"I doubt it."

He shook his head, letting me in on their game. "She'll never let me live that down."

"Can you blame her?"

He smiled at me, his eyes bright and mischievous, and my heart did some kind of acrobatic tumble in my chest. I was ridiculously aware of how close he was. It was the most physical contact we'd had since Halloween, and I was thrilled at his hand on my back and the way his hip brushed against mine. He leaned over the pan again to sniff the steam coming off the sauce. "I love the way it smells."

And I love you. The thought came unbidden, so strangely out of place and yet so strong and so true that for a moment, I forgot to stir the cranberries.

I loved him. I loved the way he smiled, and the way he teased, and the way he adored his mother. I loved everything about him, and about his family, and about the day. I felt at home. At peace. Completely whole and loved and accepted. But I couldn't say it. I couldn't put any of it into words. I concentrated instead on the sauce, on the cheery smells of sugar and cinnamon and ripe, tart fruit.

He was right. It smelled amazing. "Like Thanksgiving and Christmas all in one," I said.

His smile grew bigger. His hand lingered on my back, almost moving into a caress. For half a second, I thought he was going to kiss me in front of his mother.

I was both disappointed and relieved when he moved away.

The meal was fantastic. Afterward, we all sat around the table, too full to eat any more but not ready to nap yet either.

"I have an idea," Truvy said, turning toward June and me. "Why don't you play for us?"

"Now?" June asked.

"Why not? We'll miss the recital, but at least we'll get to hear your song."

My blood pressure began to skyrocket as it always did when I thought about the recital. "N-n-no," I stammered. But June was already grabbing my hand and pulling me toward the piano.

"This is embarrassing," I whined as we sat down on the bench.

"It is not! It's just my family. Besides, it'll be good practice. We haven't played in front of anybody but Nick and Amelia. This will be like a dress rehearsal."

It was hard to argue with that logic, no matter how much I wanted to. And so we played.

The first time through, I fumbled more than once. "See?" I hissed at June. "This is a terrible idea!"

"That was a practice run. Now we've worked out the kinks. Let's do it again." So we did, over and over throughout the rest of the day. In the end, I was glad. By the end of the night, I could sit down with June and play the song without feeling like I might hyperventilate. After that, the recital seemed marginally less frightening.

They left around nine that evening, June heading home to her own apartment and their parents for their hotel room. Nick's apartment felt surprisingly quiet and empty without them.

"I really like your family," I said.

He smiled, his eyes distant but happy, and I knew he was thinking about them. "I like them too."

"Your mom's a great cook."

He raised his eyebrows at me, teasing me. "And I'm not?"

"Your mom isn't afraid to add salt."

He laughed. "Fair enough." His smile softened. It became something gentle. "I'm glad you were here."

My heart skipped a beat, and I ducked my head, unsure how to answer. *I'm glad I'm here too. You're beautiful. Let's both stop being so lonely.* But I didn't say anything. We sat in silence, both of us staring at the TV, although I wasn't sure we were seeing it.

It was ridiculous, the way we were suddenly both so tense. We were side by side on the couch as we so often were, but I felt as if we were poised on a cliff, leaning forward, eyeing the drop. I felt the sweet call of gravity.

He put his hand on my shoulder. My heart raced as he pulled me close, against his side.

"Nick?" I whispered.

"Shhh," he soothed as he put his arms around me. He stroked my hair and kissed the top of my head. "Just this, okay? I miss it."

I closed my eyes and swallowed against the lump in my throat. How could he make me so happy and yet so sad, all at the same time?

"Is it okay?" he asked. "If you'd rather not—"

"It's good. I miss it too." I settled against him, sighing at the feel of his arms around me. The soft touch of his lips on my hair. He was strong and warm and he smelled so good. It was all heartbreakingly comfortable and familiar.

Just this.

It's enough, I thought.

For now.

THE WEATHER took a turn for the worse on the Friday after Thanksgiving, and as the skies darkened, so did Nick's mood. He seemed beaten, and I had no

idea why. He put on a good show for his family, but I
sensed the grief that lay underneath his cheery facade.
I'd felt close to him in the preceding days, but now he
was distant again, although still friendly. I wondered
if it had to do with us cuddling on the couch the night
before, but I suspected there was more to it.

Truvy seemed to sense his mood as well, and several times I saw her watching him, her anguished expression matching his. When it was time for them to
leave, he held his mother so tight I feared he'd hurt her.
I was surprised to see tears on his cheeks.

"You're coming for Christmas, right?" she asked
him as she wiped the tears away the way any good
mother would.

"I wouldn't miss it."

"You know you can bring Owen."

He nodded, but I could tell he didn't feel any better.
It confirmed what I'd already suspected—I was only a
small part of whatever was bothering him.

Truvy didn't have to wonder, though. Truvy
knew. "Honey," she said, reaching up to put her hands
on his cheeks, "*stop*. You're healthy now, and you'll
be healthy later. We're going to have plenty of other
holidays."

"We don't know that."

"*I do*," she said. She kissed him again. "I'll see you
at Christmas."

DECEMBER DESCENDED upon us with subzero
temperatures and a wet, heavy snow that stripped any
remaining leaves from the trees and brought branches
crashing to the ground. Nick and I continued to walk
his dogs every evening after dinner, shivering as we
hurried along, hugging our arms around ourselves for

warmth, but whatever camaraderie we'd shared on Thanksgiving night was gone. I began to notice the way he watched me. Sometimes I thought he was waiting for me to move closer to him, to reach for his hand, but other times he looked terrified. Sometimes, I was sure I saw relief in his eyes when I said good night.

It took me several days to get up my nerve, but one night as we sat watching TV side by side on his couch surrounded by dogs, I managed to say, "I w-wish you'd talk to me."

He didn't look at me. He barely blinked. His only movement was the slow stroke of his hand on Betty's head. "About what?"

"About what's bothering you."

"Isn't it obvious?"

"Is it just because you're sick?"

He snorted in disgust. "'Just' because? Isn't that enough of a reason?"

"But you've been so different since Thanksgiving."

He slumped, the anger he'd tried to hold against me suddenly gone. "This is always the hardest time of the year for me, between Thanksgiving and Christmas."

I could understand that to some extent. "Lots of people get depressed around the holidays."

"It's just hard for me to see my parents and wonder if I'll ever have another holiday with them."

"There's no reason to assume you won't."

"There's no reason to assume I will."

"Nick—"

"You don't get it. It's not just about me. It's about them. I was young and stupid and careless, and now I've brought this thing—this illness—into my family like some kind of curse. I feel my mother watching me and my father weighing his words."

"I think you're imagining it." Much as I'd imagined people staring at my missing arm, I realized.

He shook his head. "I'm not."

"Then that's all the more reason you should enjoy it now." I took a deep breath and reached out to take his hand. "Why *we* should enjoy it."

He pulled his hand away, and some fragile thing inside me broke. With a single gesture, he'd crushed every ounce of my hope. I hated how much it hurt. "Nick?"

"You have it backwards. Don't you see? This is exactly why it can't work between us. It's exactly why you should find somebody else. Because I can't ask you to spend every holiday with me wondering if it will be the last one."

"And what about me? I take it I have no say in the matter?"

His jaw clenched, but he didn't answer.

I couldn't pity him, though. Not this time. I'd accepted his reasoning again and again, but it wore a bit thinner each time. How did both of us being miserable make things right? How was being alone better than being happy?

I wanted to reach for him. To hold him and kiss him and comfort him. To push against his boundaries until he accepted that I could help him. But I couldn't take being rejected again.

I stood up, dislodging Betty and Bonny as I did.

"Where are you going?"

"Home."

"Why?"

"Because I'm tired of watching you act like some kind of martyr."

"Martyr?" he said, standing up to face me. "Is that what you think? You think I chose this? You think I'm doing it on purpose?"

He was angry now, but I didn't back down. I was tired of giving in. "Do you have some other explanation?"

"I didn't choose to be sick."

"No, but you choose to let it define you."

"You don't understand."

"I understand plenty. You say it's not just about you? Well, you're wrong. This *is* about you. It's about *your* issues. Not HIV, but your determination to let it dictate how you spend the rest of your life."

"You have no idea what you're talking about."

"I think I do. You've used it as an excuse to push me away time and again, but to what end, Nick? For what purpose? Just to prove how noble you are? Well, it's bullshit. You try to hide behind your family or behind claims that this is all for my own good, but the truth is you're determined to keep punishing yourself for something that happened five years ago. I'm tired of it, Nick. I'll be your friend, or I'll be your lover, but I won't be the instrument of your self-flagellation."

He turned away, hiding his expression. I didn't know if he was angry or wounded or both. At that moment I didn't care.

Chapter Eleven

As WE moved deeper into December, dread loomed over me with the black persistence of a cartoon rain cloud, dogging my steps both inside and out. With each passing day, the piano recital drew closer. And so did the visit from my parents.

My mother called a few days before they were scheduled to arrive. I hoped she was calling to cancel, but no such luck.

"Your dad told me we have to stay in a hotel."

"I only have one bed at my place, Mom. The second bedroom is my office."

"Your office? What in the world do you need an office for?"

"For m-my work."

I didn't need to see her to know she was rolling her eyes. "Really, Owen. I don't see why you can't get a real job. We didn't spend all those months practicing your typing so you could hide from the world. We did it so you could try to fit in."

I didn't bother asking what exactly made my job insufficient. I didn't bother trying to defend the fact that my second bedroom held a desk instead of a bed. I sat there listening to her complain about every aspect of my life, and I felt myself shrinking, becoming the child I'd once been, barely able to speak without stuttering.

A hundred times I thought about quitting the recital. I debated the excuses I could make to June and Amelia. I thought of lies I could tell my parents to keep them from visiting, each one more ridiculous than the last. I had the flu. I had measles. My house had been condemned. In the end, I did nothing, and time marched on.

My argument with Nick continued to weigh on me as well. I was heartsick over him. I saw him every day, and yet he was more distant than ever. I felt as if he'd deserted me. I wanted my fun, confident, flirtatious friend back. I wanted to hold his hand again. To snuggle next to him on the couch. I wanted to melt in his arms and have him kiss me. To take him to bed and give myself to him in every possible way. But I was afraid to touch him, and afraid he'd only push me away again.

The day before my parents were to arrive, I sat at Nick's piano, trying to practice. June and I had finished our lesson, and June had left for the night. Nick stood talking to Amelia for a while at his front door. I wondered only briefly what they were discussing. Anxiety kept me from mustering up too much curiosity.

I concentrated on the music.

I knew the song by heart now. I barely had to look at the keys anymore, let alone the music. Still, I stared down at the piano with unwavering concentration. "Ode to Joy," but this didn't feel like joy. It felt like terror. I wished I knew how to play something mournful. Something that fit my mood.

I looked up as Nick came into the room. He straddled the bench and sat facing me. It was something he'd never done before, and my fingers missed a note. My heart began to pound, and I stumbled to a halt. I sat still under the weight of his gaze, too depressed to hope for anything.

"Two days away," he said.

"I'm not ready."

"Yes, you are. You'll do great."

"I'm scared."

"Of what? Playing in the recital?"

"That too. But mostly I'm afraid of my mom." I felt like I'd made tremendous progress since meeting Nick, and I was sure a few days with her would destroy it all.

When I finally turned to face Nick, I saw sympathy in his eyes. He hesitated for a moment, and then he reached toward me. He brushed his fingers down my cheek. "Whatever happens, I'm here for you. You know that, right?"

I swallowed hard, suddenly afraid to speak. I took in the sorrow in his eyes and the lines on his face betraying his own depression. I ached for him. After his confession on Halloween, I'd worried that I'd always see him as Nick Who Was Dying of HIV, but the virus had long since fallen into the background where it belonged. It didn't define him any more than my missing arm defined me. He was still Nick. Nick the veterinarian who would risk his lease to give one more dog a home and who volunteered his services to the local humane society. Nick who was confident and strong and sexy as hell, who ate more broiled fish than anybody I knew and railed against the evils of Halloween candy. Nick whom I loved so much I wasn't sure how my heart could hold it all.

But now he was Nick who felt beyond my reach. Nick who would never hold me again, or kiss me. Nick who would never share my bed. And it wasn't because of the virus. It was because of my ignorance and his ridiculous stubbornness. My knee-jerk reaction to his illness and his goddamn martyr-like determination to protect me, whether I wanted it or not.

I reached for him, wanting more than anything to tell him I didn't want to be protected anymore. To feel his arms around me and the solid comfort of his body against mine. But I was too slow. Whether he knew my intentions or not, he stood up…

And he walked away.

"I'VE NEVER liked Colorado."

That was the first thing my mother said to me as she walked through my front door. We hadn't seen each other in four years, and that was the best greeting she could muster.

"What's wrong with it?"

She shed her coat and handed it to me to deal with. "I thought maybe the Western Slope would be prettier than the Front Range, but they look the same to me."

I hung her coat on one of the hooks by the door. "It's gorgeous here, actually. If you saw it in spring or summer or even fall—" I stopped, realizing my mistake. I'd just made it sound as if it was her fault for coming at the wrong time of year.

She sniffed, looking away from me. "The traffic across I-70 was horrendous. Really, Owen, I don't see why you had to leave Laramie at all."

"I think it's charming," my dad said as he pulled me into a hug. "It suits you."

"Thanks, Dad. You found the hotel all right? You're all checked in?"

"Yep, no problems at all. It seems like a real nice place."

"The first room they gave us reeked of cigarette smoke," my mom said. "I called and complained, and they moved us to a new room, but it smells as bad as the other one did."

My dad's smile was tight, stuck to his face like a plastic Halloween mask, brittle and unreal. "Well, it'll only be two days. I think we'll manage."

I ordered dinner in that night. Nick had offered to cook for us. In fact, he'd offered to be with me every minute of my time with my mother, but I'd refused. I didn't want him to see me with her. I didn't want him to witness the humiliation and disdain she poured on me with every breath, although he made a point of coming upstairs to meet them.

My dad was genuinely friendly and enthusiastic in his greeting, but my mother was characteristically reserved.

"I hope you're not too close to him," she said to me, once he was gone and we were settling at the kitchen table to eat.

"Wh-why is th-that?"

"Think about it. A good-looking young man like that, and yet he's not married?" Her lips twisted in disgust. "He's probably one of *them*. The last thing you need is to be mixed up with people who are bad influences in that regard."

"He's a n-n-nice person, Mom."

"Well, we know all a boy has to do is pretend he likes you and you'll do anything. Just like with Jeremy Brewer."

My cheeks flushed hot with humiliation. It was so typical of her to throw the incident with Jeremy in my face. Yes, he'd acted like my friend. He'd kissed me and touched me, but when we were caught under the bleachers, breathless in each other's arms, he'd turned his back on me. Nick would never do that.

And yet the seed of doubt my mother had sown was there, under the muck of my shame. He had pushed me away time and again. Maybe it wasn't about the HIV or his ridiculous sense of nobility. Maybe I really was as pathetic as my mother said.

"What is this, anyway?" my mother asked, looking through the delivery cartons on the table. "It smells terrible."

"I thought you liked Chinese food."

"I like *good* Chinese food." She pushed it away. "I don't see why we can't go out."

"Owen's already paid for this," my dad said. "Anyway, we came here to see Owen, remember? To spend some time with our son."

"And we can't spend time with him and have a decent meal at the same time?"

"Restaurants are so noisy, Valerie. Especially on Fridays. This is more intimate."

It was a nice attempt, but nothing could salvage my dignity. The food tasted like dirt in my mouth. I could barely stand to swallow. Through it all, my dad attempted to make small talk, asking me about Tucker Springs, my work, my friends. No matter what subject we landed on, my mother continued to ooze contempt.

"And now you're learning to play piano!" my dad said with a smile. "It's wonderful."

"It's ridiculous is what it is," my mother mumbled.

My father ignored her. "Tell me about this girl you're playing in the recital with."

It was no use, though. My answers became more and more muddled, my tongue heavier with each tick of the clock. When they finally stood up to leave, I nearly wept with relief.

"How about if we all go downtown tomorrow?" my dad said at the door. "We can have lunch first, and then you can spend some time showing us around before the recital."

It was the last thing in the world I wanted to do, but arguing would have meant speaking.

Only one more day, I told myself. *One day with them, then play the recital, and then they'll go home and everything will go back to normal.*

The problem was, I didn't know what normal was.

THE NEXT morning dawned bright and bone-jarringly frigid. Clear winter days were often the coldest in Colorado, and this one seemed determined to prove a point. The air felt sharp and angry against my bare cheeks as I led my parents through the Light District.

I took them to the Vibe for lunch because it was the only restaurant in the area I was familiar with. I knew my mother would hate it, but I couldn't come up with anyplace she *wouldn't* hate.

She glanced around with obvious disapproval. "Is that macramé?" She wrinkled her nose in disgust at the wide jute hanging that separated the counter from the seating area. "Looks like it's been there since the seventies. I bet it's never been cleaned either. Just think of all the dust mites that must live in it."

"I'd prefer to think of no such thing," my dad mumbled.

I stuttered through my order, feeling my mother's judgmental gaze on the back of my neck. My father and I barely spoke through the meal, but my mother talked plenty. The bread was too dry, the fries too soggy. The fish tanks smelled bad and the bathrooms were too dirty. My whole life it had been this way. My mother could never see the sun. She only saw shadows, no matter where she turned. After that, it was back out into the deceptively bright, sunny day.

"Y-y-you should s-see it at n-night," I told them as we walked through the Light District. "They t-turn on all the l-l-lights, and when the w-w-weather's good, they have f-free c-concerts over th-there in the amphitheater."

"Sounds like a waste of electricity."

Her negativity was never-ending. Nothing met her approval. When El waved at me through his shop window, she sneered. "What a horrible little store." And when Seth stepped out of his door to call after me, "That offer still stands, Owen!" she turned to me with obvious horror.

"For God's sake, Owen. Please tell me you're not getting tattoos now."

"N-n-no, M-Mom. It was j-j-j—"

"People get AIDS at places like that, you know. Heaven knows how many people they've infected."

"Th-th-they don't m-m-m-make p-p-p-p—" *They don't make people sick.* That's what I wanted to say. *They're smart. They're careful. They're regulated!* The words built up behind my tongue like water against a dam, but they couldn't break free. There was no way to have them heard without them tumbling over each other, making me sound like a fool.

"Don't try to defend them," my mom interrupted. "I see all the rainbow flags in the windows. I'm not stupid. I know what that means. This is where the gays live. I suppose if they get AIDS, it's only what they deserve."

"Sh-sh-shut up, Mom! You d-d-don't know anything!"

"I know you're living here in this neighborhood with that boy downstairs. You play piano at his house. I'm not blind."

"Valerie, that's enough," my dad said.

"It's indecent. That's all. Do you ever think about us at all? About what people will *say*?"

Anger welled up in me, hot and vile and cruel. "W-why should I, M-Mom? D-do you ever think about *me*? Do you h-h-have any idea how m-m-miserable you've m-made me my entire life? Do you even c-care?"

She pulled herself together, shoulders thrust back and her spine rigid. "Stop it, Owen. Listen to yourself. You don't even know what you're saying."

But she was wrong. I knew exactly what I was saying. "I am gay, M-M-Mom. Just like them. And I w-won't apologize for it. Especially not to y-you."

I left them standing there, my mother shocked and angry, my father calling for me to come back. I ignored him.

We'd come downtown in my parents' car, but I wasn't about to wait for them to catch up. I decided to walk home, despite the cold. I felt broken and defeated, shattered into a million little pieces by my mother's cruel indifference. She'd done just as I'd feared, taken all of my newfound confidence and crushed it beneath her heel. But this time I knew how to get it back. There was one person who could always help me put myself back together, and right now I wanted him more than ever.

Chapter Twelve

IT WAS all I could do to hold myself together until Nick answered the door, but the minute he did, I felt better. The dogs swarmed around my feet, begging for attention, but I ignored them. I grabbed Nick with my one good hand and pulled him toward me.

"Don't tell me no. Not today."

I didn't give him time to protest. I kissed him instead, hard and insistent, putting every ounce of my frustration into it. I was broken, and I wanted him to help fix me. I wanted him to feel my urgency. To know how much I needed him and to accept the fact that he needed me too. Because he did. Whether he was ready to admit it or not, I knew in my heart that I filled an empty space in his life, just as he did for me. I'd had enough of his foolish nobility and his excuses. He made me happy in a way nobody else ever had. I wanted to do the same for him. I begged him with my kiss to give me that chance.

He hesitated for a moment, but then he put his arms around my waist and he kissed me back.

Everything changed in the moment when his tongue touched mine. Every bit of restraint he'd held on to disappeared. It was frantic and primal, weeks' worth of attraction and denial overflowing, driving us at each other, tearing down the walls.

This was what I wanted—to be with him. To have my desire returned. To have the horrible empty place inside me filled by his tenderness. To know that I was safe and cared for and understood. I didn't care about the virus or my mother's horrible words. I loved Nick. I belonged with Nick. And right now, at this moment, I wanted to shed our clothes. To lock the doors and let the world die a frozen death while we reveled in our heat. I wanted to feel his body hard and naked and heavy on mine.

He let me guide him into the bedroom and pull him down on the bed. He let me wrap my legs around him, holding him tighter than my arms ever could. But when I reached for the buttons of his pants, he jerked away from me, panting.

"Owen, I can't. We can't do this."

"Yes, we can."

"You know I'm HIV-positive—"

"Yes, I *know*. That's the point. And I don't care. There are no more secrets between us." I pulled his pants open and slid my hand inside to cup his erection through his underwear. The proof of his desire was in my hand, hard against my palm. It was in his eyes and his labored breath. It was in the way he held me and the way he moaned as I began to rub his bulge.

"I need this," I told him. "And I think you do too."

My poor Nick. He tried so hard to be noble, but he wasn't that strong. Not when it came to this. He moaned, not just with pleasure, but with the grief of knowing he couldn't win. The frustration of admitting his desire was stronger than his will. Maybe it was wrong of me to push him when I knew the depths of his struggles, but I didn't want to coddle him. Not this time.

I pulled the waistband of his underwear out of the way. I felt him give in, surrendering himself to the inevitable, as his erection popped free. It was the sweetest victory I'd ever won, and I wrapped my fist around his cock and stroked. His breath caught. A flash of euphoria flitted across his face, but then he grabbed my wrist and pulled my hand away. He lay shuddering on top of me, his breath hot against my neck.

"It's been a long time, Owen." His voice trembled, but he seemed more embarrassed than anything. "A *really* long time."

"Don't tell me I can't touch you. Not tonight."

He laughed shakily. "I'm not saying you can't, but you better stop now if you want this to last more than three minutes."

I laughed too, but it excited me knowing I had this kind of power over him. "Do you have some kind of lubricant?"

"We can't have sex. We can't—"

"I know what I'm doing."

He hesitated for a moment, debating, but then he let go of me. I kept my legs wrapped around his hips as he reached into the bottom drawer of his bedside table and came up with a tube. I held my hand out, and he squirted some onto my palm. The whole thing had taken only a couple of seconds, and when I wrapped my hand around his cock again, he groaned. He closed his eyes and thrust into my fist. He shuddered and pulled me close, burying his face against my neck.

"Owen," he whispered. "Jesus, I think three minutes might have been wishful thinking."

I kissed his coarse cheek, stroked my fist down his length to feel him shudder again. "Go ahead," I whispered. "I've got you."

His first thrust was hesitant, as if testing his own restraint. The second was slow and deliberate, and I watched him, thrilled at the ecstasy I saw on his face. His next thrust was harder, and he opened his eyes to look down at me. I could see the desperation in them, a plea for me to still be okay with what he was doing.

I smiled at him. "I've got you," I said again.

He made a sound, something between a moan and a growl, a noise so primal and so powerful it made my heart race and my groin ache. It was the sound of desperation and need, of finally letting go, of giving in to his lust. He began humping his hips, fucking my fist with an abandon that bordered on violence. His cock was hot and slick as my fingers slid over his glans again and again. Every muscle in his body went taut. His fingers dug painfully into my sides. He panted and grunted into my neck as he rutted into my hand.

I'd wanted him to make love to me, but that wasn't what this was. At this moment, I could have been anyone. This wasn't about me. It was about him. It was five years of sexual frustration finally set free, and I was happy to be the one to give it to him. All my worries and insecurities fled as I gave him the thing he needed most at that moment. He chased his pleasure, driving into me harder and harder until he came, roaring with the strength of his release, emptying himself onto my stomach. He collapsed on top of me, panting and shaking, and I held him against me as best as I could with both arms.

"Owen," he finally said into my ear. "That wasn't very generous of me."

"I don't mind."

"I didn't mean for it to go like that."

"I liked it," I said, turning to kiss his cheek. "I liked getting to be the hero for once."

He laughed. "I liked it too, but I think I can do better." He sat up to look down at us—his pants gaping, his drooping cock hanging free—and the sticky mess he'd made on my T-shirt. "How about if we clean up a bit?"

We undressed each other, and I let him lead me into the shower. There, under a scalding spray, he pulled me into his arms. He took my erection in his hand. "Your turn."

I wanted to lose myself in him completely, the way he'd lost himself with me. I wanted to let him be the hero this time, but that wasn't how it felt. As the water fell over us and the bathroom filled with steam, he kissed me and stroked me, but he was already pulling away. There were no sweet, whispered words. Only reservations and a lingering sense of embarrassment. I felt abandoned. I could almost taste his regret. I knew by the pinched look around his eyes he was already beating himself up for allowing me to touch him. By the time it was over, the water was turning cold. I stood shivering as he found me a towel. He couldn't quite meet my eyes.

"It'll be time to go soon," he said to me when I came out of the bathroom. "You probably want to change."

"Can I ride with you?"

He nodded, but he didn't smile at me. Whatever pleasure we'd had together, he was paying the price for it now. I could see the guilt on his face, the lines of worry around his eyes.

"Nick, please don't do this."

He pinched the top of his nose and shook his head. "I have no self-control with you."

"Good."

"No. It's not good. If you get sick because of me, I'll never forgive myself."

I didn't know if I was hurt or angry. I couldn't decide if I wanted to burst into tears or to rail at him for making things so hard. I either wanted to pull him into my arms and let him come apart, or beat him until he gave up being so goddamn stubborn. In the end, I didn't get to decide because my cell phone rang. One glance at the caller ID was enough to make me cringe.

"Hello?"

I'd hoped it might be my dad on the line, but no such luck. "Owen, are you sure about this? There's still time to back out."

"I'm not quitting."

She sighed heavily. "I think we'd all be better off staying inside. It's so cold out, and the roads are icy. I'm afraid your dad will wreck the car."

"You're from Wyoming, Mom. It's not like Dad doesn't know how to handle a bit of snow on the roads."

"Are the pews padded? It's not one of those churches that has wooden benches, is it? Or those metal folding chairs? I don't know if my back can take—"

And in that moment, I broke. I'd had enough. Enough of Nick's tug-of-war. Enough of my mother's complaints. Enough of living my life according to the dictates of other people.

"Then don't come."

She instantly fell silent. I could sense her disapproval and her indignation at being cut off. At being dismissed. "Well, if that's the way you feel—"

"It is. I'm tired of listening to you talk about the son you wished you'd had. I'm the one you've got, Mom, and if you don't want to be there for me, it's no skin off my nose. I never wanted you here in the first place."

I'd finally done it. I'd rid myself of my mother's venomous attitude, and I hadn't stuttered even once while I'd done it. I hung up, feeling victorious, and turned to find Nick watching me, his eyes wide.

"Good for you," he said.

But I wasn't in the mood to be congratulated. I was just as tired of his well-intentioned martyrdom as I was of my mother's attitude. "Are you going to apologize and tell me we're fine, or are you going to keep pretending like you have to push me away to be noble?"

"Owen, you don't understand—"

"I understand a lot better than you think. Frankly, I think I understand it better than you." I felt his eyes on me as I dressed, but I didn't shrink under the weight of his confusion. "You haven't broken out of that cage as much as you like to think."

"Owen, wait," he called as I headed for the door. "Don't you need a ride?"

"I'd rather walk."

I HAD to run upstairs before I left to put on a clean shirt and warmer coat. It was still cold out, and although I was already regretting the way I'd left things with Nick, I didn't regret turning down the ride. I could have taken my own car, but walking to the recital gave me time to think.

First and foremost, I thought about my mother. My whole life I'd thought I was the focus of her anger, but now, looking back on the day, I began to realize it wasn't just me. My friends and the town. The restaurant and the tattoo parlor. Nothing escaped her disdain.

Had it always been that way?

I remembered all the vile things she'd said to me over the years, but this time I made myself think beyond them. I thought back to Easter Sundays and Thanksgivings when she'd complained of the work and the mess. Christmas mornings when she'd moaned that nobody had bothered to get her anything nice. Vacations where everything was wrong from the flight to the hotel to the swimsuit-invading sand at the beach.

My mother had never once been happy, and with the narcissism of a child, I'd assumed it was because of me. But I realized now with a sudden, blinding clarity, it wasn't.

It was because of *her*.

Such a simple revelation, but it was liberating. I wasn't responsible for her or her foul disposition. The realization felt so momentous that I laughed out loud. So many years of trying to please her, and for what? Just to give her more ammunition to throw my way?

Not anymore. It was over. Never again would I question myself because of her.

I was free.

My first thought was how I wished Nick were with me. I wished I could tell him what I'd learned, share my victory with him, but hot on the heels of that thought came a wave of sadness. I'd pushed my way into Nick's apartment, needing him like never before, and he'd delivered. But as soon as it was over, he'd pulled away again.

The night suddenly felt colder, and I hugged myself with my good arm.

Maybe I'd been wrong to push him. Maybe I'd been selfish. And yet I was sure he needed me as much as I needed him. Maybe more. We loved each other. We belonged together. I knew it deep in my heart, but I had no idea how to deal with his thickheadedness. The only thing I could do was continue beating at the ridiculously noble intentions he shielded himself with. They were stupid and pointless, but he held on to them so tightly. I wanted to rip them away and shine a light on them, reveal them for what they really were—a way for him to punish himself for a mistake he'd made in his youth. It was infuriating and exhausting, and I wasn't sure how many more times I could swallow the pain of rejection.

I sighed, unable to reclaim the glory of having told off my mother. I felt more lost than ever.

I rounded the corner and saw the church ahead of me, its lights twinkling in the dark like some kind of beacon, but whether of damnation and salvation, I couldn't be sure. Thoughts of my mother and Nick began to fade into the background. The reality of what was to come became clear in my mind, my sole point of focus. Fear blossomed in my stomach. Not the mindless panic I would have felt two months earlier, but a nervous kind of excitement that made my stomach buzz and my heart pound.

I can do this. But even in my mind, I balked, so I said the words out loud. "I can do this." It helped.

A little.

Nick had driven, and so of course he'd beaten me to the church. I found him waiting for me by the door. I stopped in front of him, still angry, still confused, but also scared and badly in need of reassurance.

He smiled as he held the door open for me, although the happiness of it didn't quite reach his eyes. "You'll do fine."

"Where have you guys been?" June said when we walked in. She was a twitchy bundle of nerves. It didn't help soothe my own growing anxiety.

"Just running late," I said.

"Well, come on! They'll be starting any minute!"

I glanced around as we found our seats. My mother was nowhere to be seen. I'd expected that, but I didn't see my father either. Nathan was there, though, waving at me from the back of the room. It made me nervous, having him there, but it felt great too, knowing he'd come just to support me.

June, Nick, and I found an open space big enough for the three of us on one of the cold, hard pews. I sat with Nick on my left and June on my right. I looked up at the piano sitting at the front of the room. I looked around at the many, many faces. All the people who would see me walk to the front of the room, amputated arm and all. All the people who would hear me play.

Maybe my mother was right. Maybe I should quit.

No. Not now. You can do this.

Beginning students went first, which should have worked to our advantage, but Amelia had decided to put all the duets later in the program, before the more advanced students played their pieces. Three other students played "Ode to Joy." All three were kids. All fumbled, but not terribly, and I noticed that the audience clapped for them just the same. June reached out and took hold of my hand.

As our turn drew near, the nerves that had taken root began to feel like something much bigger. Something so real and alive it might swallow me whole. What if we messed up? What if I forgot the notes? What if, when we finished the piece, nobody clapped at all?

What if they laughed?

"These next students have only been with me for two and half months now," Amelia said, and I knew it was our turn. "Their progress has been remarkable, all the more so because of their unique special circumstances." I winced, unsure how I felt about her introduction. I looked to gauge June's reaction, but before I could, I felt Nick's strong, warm hand on my shoulder.

I turned to face him. I wanted to say so many things to him, but this wasn't the time. He still looked guilty. He still looked sad. But he offered me a smile. "I'm proud of you, no matter what. You're going to do great."

Twenty minutes ago, I'd wanted to strangle him. Now all I wanted was to hear him say those words again.

I'd missed the next bit of Amelia's introduction. I tuned in again in time to hear her say, "June Reynolds and Owen Meade."

I rose on unsteady legs, and June and I walked hand in hand toward the front of the auditorium. The crowd seemed to draw breath as one, and then a quiet wave of whispers washed over them.

They're talking about us. The two one-armed piano players.

"Mommy," some kid said, her theatrical whisper far too loud in the quiet room, "what happened to their arms?"

I heard the sharp hiss of her mother trying to hush her. "We don't ask questions like that, Annabelle!" I felt the discomfort of the crowd. Leave it to a child to point to the elephant in the room.

I thought about stopping. I thought about turning to the audience, about searching for Annabelle, about telling her mom, "It's okay." But there was no time, and I wasn't that brave.

We took our seat at the piano, and we played.

It was both horrifying and exhilarating. My fingers seemed to move on their own. My foot worked the pedal. Next to me, June watched her fingers with unwavering concentration. I fumbled once, and so did she, but both mistakes were quick, and we recovered easily.

It felt good. "Ode to Joy," I thought, and I found myself smiling. This *was* joy, creating music from nothing. Sitting next to June. Knowing Nathan was here for me and Nick was waiting for me, one way or another, as a lover or a friend. I had no idea what was going to happen between us. I only knew that I wanted more of this feeling—joy. I'd been missing it my whole life, and now, having lived with it for a moment or two, I never wanted to let it go.

But almost as quickly as it had begun, the song ended.

June and I sat in the sudden silence, staring at the mute keys.

"We did it!" I said.

June smiled at me, but whatever she was about to say was lost to the deafening sound of applause. We turned as one to face the crowd, and my jaw dropped.

They'd clapped for everybody, but this time they were on their feet. They were cheering and shouting. Did we deserve this extra attention just because of our arms? Part of me wanted to say no, but then June pulled me to my feet. We faced the crowd, and she bowed as if this were Carnegie Hall. As if we really were stars. Or heroes.

And all I could do was laugh.

THE LAST half of the recital went by in a blur. I barely heard the advanced students as they played their pieces. I leaned close to Nick. He reached across my lap to hold my hand.

Joy.

When it was over, everybody gathered in the foyer, smiling and congratulating each other.

"Absolutely brilliant!" Nathan raved, pounding me on the back.

An obvious exaggeration, but I didn't mind. My dad found me shortly afterward and pulled me into a tight hug. "You were amazing, son."

"I didn't know you were here. Did you hear me play?"

"I wouldn't have missed it."

He let me go and I looked around for my mom, but I already knew what I'd find.

"We need to talk," my dad said, suddenly somber. "How about if I give you a lift? We can have a heart-to-heart at your place over some hot chocolate?"

"Sure, Dad."

I couldn't tell if Nick was disappointed or relieved when I told him I had a ride home. I had a feeling he wasn't sure either. I waved goodbye to Nathan and June and headed for the door with my father. We were half-way there when a red-faced woman ushered her pig-tailed daughter up to me.

"I want to apologize," she said. "Annabelle didn't mean—"

"It's fine," I said, and I was surprised to realize it was true. I didn't mind. "It's normal for kids to be curious." I looked down at the girl. She couldn't have been more than four. How could she understand? I crouched down to face her. "You can ask," I said.

She glanced up at her mom, unsure. The mother was clearly uncomfortable, but she nodded. Annabelle looked back at me. "Where's your arm?" Blunt, just like Nick. It made me smile.

"I've never had one. When I was in my mommy's tummy, something went wrong, and my arm never grew." Not exactly correct, but close enough for somebody as young as her.

"What went wrong?"

"It's called an amniotic band."

"Like a rubber band?"

"Yes, actually. Similar to a rubber band."

"Did your mom swallow one?"

"Well, no—"

"One time I put a rubber band around my finger, and it started to turn blue, and Mommy said don't do that 'cause of circle nation."

She was so solemn. I did my best not to laugh. "Circulation?"

"Circle-ation."

"That's exactly right. That's what happened, but when I was still in my mom's tummy."

She looked with unabashed curiosity at my stump. "Does it hurt?"

"Not at all."

"Can I touch it?"

"If you want."

She reached out and pinched the rounded end of my arm. Whatever she'd been curious about, she nodded, obviously satisfied. "Good. Tell your mommy, don't swallow rubber bands."

This time, I really did laugh. "I will."

Chapter Thirteen

WE WERE halfway home before the heat started to work in my dad's car. He cleared his throat a lot as he drove, which told me that whatever he wanted to talk about, it made him nervous.

"I can't believe Mom didn't come," I said. It was a bit of a lie, but it seemed like the right thing to say.

My father winced. "I can't believe a lot of the things your mother does."

I'd never heard my dad say anything negative about my mom, and yet when I thought back, I realized I'd never really heard him defend her either. Whenever she tossed one of her thoughtless comments my way, my dad had been there, patting me on the back, offering to take me out for ice cream.

You'll make him fat, my mom had said on more than one occasion.

But not once did my dad heed her.

Back at my place, I put a pan on the stove and filled it with milk. I stirred it until it frothed around the edges. I got out the mugs and the mix, and the entire time, I thought about my childhood. I thought about how I'd spent so many years trying to please my mom, and all along my dad had watched in silence, bringing me little gifts behind her back.

My dad took his cocoa, and I took mine, and we sat at the dinner table. My dad cupped his mug between his palms, letting the heat warm them. I thought about June saying it was the only thing she'd ever missed about not having a right hand. I thought about all the times I'd seen my father do it, bending over his mug to let the steam tickle his nose.

"We used to do this when I was a kid," I said at last, breaking the silence. "And Mom always said, 'You'll ruin his dinner.'"

He nodded. "Or, if it was after dinner, she'd say, 'You'll make him wet the bed.'"

"What? I never wet the bed!"

"I know." He took a sip of his cocoa and set it down carefully, as if it were easier to concentrate on not spilling than on facing me. "I've asked your mother for a divorce."

"What? When?"

"This afternoon, after we got back to our hotel. I know it probably comes as a shock, but only because we've kept so many things from you." He shook his head. "I owe you an apology, Owen. And an explanation."

"For what?"

"For everything." He took a deep breath. I could tell he was gearing up to tell me everything, so I waited until he was ready. "I didn't date your mother very long before we got married. Even when she was young, she wasn't a pleasant person. I'd actually already broken things off with her when she told me she was pregnant."

"So you married her."

"Back then, that was what you did."

"But...." I thought back to what I knew. "You guys were together several years before I was born."

He nodded. "She lost the baby six months later. Went into labor early and delivered, but the baby was dead." He shook his head. "It was awful. Even then, I don't think I loved your mother much, but I'd already learned to love that baby, and then to have her die, it was devastating for both of us."

"I can't imagine."

"I wish our grief had driven us closer together, but it didn't. It only drove us apart. And a couple of years later, I had an affair." He looked up at me, his eyes full of guilt. "With a man."

Just when I thought he couldn't shock me more than he already had. "You're gay?"

"No." He sighed and put his head in his hands. "Bisexual, maybe. I don't know."

"How can you not know?"

"It was different then. There was no such thing as 'out and proud.' Not in our town, at any rate."

"Did you love him?"

"Maybe."

"Who was he?"

He dropped his hands from his face, but he didn't meet my eyes. He rubbed his thumb over a water stain on my tabletop. "The father of one of my students. He was married too. It was wrong no matter how you look at it. When your mom found out, she lost it. She was furious. I halfway hoped she'd want a divorce, but she cared more about our reputation than anything else."

"You could have left her."

"That's probably how it seems, but that's not how it felt. She threatened to out me, and to out him. He was a doctor." He stopped to take a sip of his cocoa. "We would have both lost our jobs. We would have lost everything. He chose to go back to his wife, and so did I."

"What happened?"

"After that, I did my best to behave… well, the way she expected me to, if you know what I mean. To be a, umm"—he blushed—"an attentive husband. But I kept thinking about how miserable I was with her, wondering if I could leave her. If I could stand to leave town and go someplace new and start over on my own. But a few months later your mom was pregnant again. With you."

"And you were trapped."

He shook his head, but I could see the truth in his eyes.

"You must have hated me."

"No!" His tone was strong, and he finally met my gaze again. "I may have resented you a bit when you were still in her womb, but once you were born…." He smiled at me. "How could I do anything but love you? And especially when I saw the way your mom acted, the way she seemed to blame you for not being born perfect." He shook his head. "I think she was punishing you for being my son more than anything. I'd hurt her, and she wanted to hurt me back however she could. So I knew I had to stay. I had to protect you. I wanted to protect you. The thing is, I'm not sure I did a very good job."

"You know, up until today, I actually thought it was only me she was awful to."

He laughed. "Oh, it's not just you, believe me. Your mom hates everything. She's an angry, bitter woman. She always has been. I don't know what happened to make her that way, but I know better than anybody. She thrives on putting others down so she can lift herself up."

"I always thought I could fix it, like, 'if I get good grades, if I can just stop stuttering, if I only had both arms.'"

"You and me both. For me it was, 'if I buy her a new dress, a new car, a new house.' I wish I knew why. I wish I knew what happened to make her so angry. I know it wasn't easy for her growing up. Her parents fought a lot. Still, it's hard to imagine how anybody can be so bitter all the time. But after thirty-five years of marriage, I've finally learned that she will never be happy, no matter what I do. Nothing's ever good enough." He'd been speaking cautiously before, but now, he was winding up, speaking faster and louder, giving voice to his anger for the first time. "She hated the old house, so I bought her a new one. But right away she started complaining. It's too hot upstairs and too cold down. We can't open the windows because it'll aggravate her allergies, but the air conditioner gives her a headache. We have this great little breakfast nook, and I'd sit there in the morning and read the paper while I drank my coffee, and I'd watch the rabbits run around the backyard. But then she realized I was actually enjoying it, so she bought heavy drapes for that room, and I'm not allowed to open them because the wallpaper will fade. I don't dress right. I don't eat right. I don't talk right. We haven't slept in the same room for nearly ten years, and she still complains about my snoring. She hates every. Single. Thing. She got some kid fired from the grocery store last week because she didn't like the way the poor girl bagged her groceries, for God's sake. She's a miserable person, Owen. She's not happy unless she's unhappy. I've had people say, 'I can't believe anybody could truly be that negative,' and I want to invite them to walk a mile in my shoes just to show them it's true. I want to tell them to spend five minutes on Twitter, and they'll realize the world is full of horrible, petty people like her. The difference is, I can't just mute her or un-follow. I have to live with her day after day after day."

I almost laughed. "Wow, Dad. Tell me how you really feel."

He gave me a reluctant chuckle, but his amuse-ment didn't last. He began to worry at the stain on my table again rather than meet my eyes. "The thing is, I should have done more to shield you from her when you were growing up. Once, when you were ten, I talk-ed to a divorce attorney, but he told me I'd never be awarded custody. I was working fifty-hour weeks, and your mom was home. The courts almost always gave custody to the mothers back then, and unless I could prove she physically abused you, divorcing her would have meant leaving you with her."

"I'm sorry."

"Jesus, Owen, don't feel bad for me, please. I can't stand that. I've failed you. Over and over again, I failed you. I saw the way she berated you. The way she hurt you. The way she made your stutter worse by hounding you and humiliating you, and every time I tried to defend you, she'd get angrier and more hateful. Sometimes I wondered if my leaving would actually help. Maybe then she'd start seeing you as *her* son in-stead of *mine*, but I didn't want to leave you. And after that incident in high school with the Brewer boy." He shook his head. "If I had it to do over, I'd have taken you. I'd have kidnapped my own son and snuck away in the night, but I—" His voice broke, and his words fell away. He took a ragged breath. "I was a coward. And I'm sorry."

I thought about it all—about how he'd wanted to help but not known how. About how miserable I'd been. And yet now, I wasn't sure it mattered.

I looked around my apartment.

My apartment.

I'd finished school. I'd beaten my stutter. I'd finally beaten my mother too. I'd escaped. And although I'd wasted more of my adult years than I liked to admit trying to find a way to please her, it was over now. I had a life that was in no way dependent upon her or her approval.

I had joy.

My dad sniffled, wiping tears from his cheeks. I reached out and put my hand on top of his. "I'm fine, Dad. I really am."

He beamed up at me. He turned his hand in mine to squeeze my fingers. "I see that, son. I want you to know, I'm proud of you. I always have been, but never more than today. Never more than when I saw you walk to the front of that church. You have a good job here. A good life." His smile turned hesitant. "And if I don't miss my guess, you have a boyfriend downstairs who's crazy about you."

I blushed furiously. "I'm not sure about that."

"I am. I see the way he watches you."

"Things with Nick are…." Confusing? A disaster? Hard to explain?

"Complicated?"

"Yes."

"It seems like the worthwhile things always are." He put his hand on my shoulder, giving weight to his words. "Owen, let me give you some advice. You can spend a lifetime being miserable, and all you'll have later is regrets. But happiness? I don't think you'll ever regret that." He hooked his hand behind my neck and pulled me closer. He kissed me on the forehead. "Be happy, son. Whatever it takes."

I SPENT all night thinking about what my dad had said. It was simple and yet profound.

Be happy.

I'd spent my life being miserable—fearing my mom, being embarrassed by my arm, hiding in my apartment like some kind of criminal. I'd convinced myself that I didn't deserve to have a life.

But I did. Not only that, I deserved to be happy.

And next morning, I had a plan.

At 10:00 a.m., I was pounding on Nick's door.

He'd just come from the shower. His hair was wet. He wore only sweats. His smile was uncertain. He was so gorgeous I could have eaten him with a spoon, but I tried to tame my raging hormones.

"Hey." He was acting wary, after the way we'd left things, but he let me in. "How'd things go with your dad last night?"

"Really well."

"Good."

We stood there for a moment, silent and awkward.

"I have a present for you," he said suddenly. I followed him into the dining room. He picked something up from the piano bench and handed it to me.

It was piano music. Several different pieces and different composers, but with one thing in common—they were all written for the right hand alone. I looked up at him in surprise. "Where did you get these?"

"Online. I've been doing some research. It turns out there's a lot of piano music written for one hand. The thing is, they assume it's because your other hand is injured, and since most people are right-handed, most injuries happen to the right hand, which means most of the music is written for the left."

"I never would have thought of that."

"Me neither. But there are exceptions to the rule, of course."

"Thank you."

"I showed them to Amelia—"

"That's what you were talking to her about!"

"She said it would take practice, but that she's never had a student as dedicated as you. She said she had no doubt that by next year's recital, you'll be able to play something by yourself."

"What about June?"

He laughed. "Well, the truth is, she's a bit of a flake when it comes to things like this. She did the recital, but don't be surprised if she finds an excuse to quit in the next couple of months."

I flipped through the music. Most of it looked too hard, but a few of them looked possible.

"The thing is," Nick said, his voice suddenly quiet, "I don't want to see you quit. I like hearing you play. I like—"

He stopped short, and I dropped the music on the piano bench in order to face him.

"You like what?"

"I like having you here."

"I like being here."

He took a deep, quavering breath. "Owen, please don't make this more difficult than it needs to be."

"You're the one making it difficult, not me."

"It's just that I want you to keep playing because I think you love it—"

"I think you love me."

He ducked his head. "I do. But it's not that simple."

"It's exactly that simple."

"Owen—"

"Coincidentally enough, I've been doing some research too. And I have a gift for you." I pulled out the box of condoms I'd hidden in my coat pocket and placed it in his hand.

He stared down at it for a long time while I took off my coat and toed my shoes off. When I turned to face him again, his cheeks were red. There was also a tent forming in his sweats.

"It's too dangerous."

"No, it's not."

"You don't want this disease."

"You're right, I don't. But I do want you, and I'm tired of letting you push me away. I'm tired of letting you decide who gets to be happy and who doesn't."

"Is that really what I'm doing?"

"You were, but it's stopping now. It's stopping to-day." I stepped closer to him. I let my hand play over his growing erection as I brushed my lips over his.

"I don't know, Owen—"

"Stop arguing and tell me this: Wouldn't you like to bottom again? Wouldn't you like to lie flat on your stomach and be fucked?"

His breath caught. He moaned, a sound of dismay, but of surrender too. I couldn't help but smile.

"I thought so."

I took his hand and he let me lead him into the bedroom. He watched me undress. I'd never seen him look so uncertain.

"This is a bad idea."

"Shut up." I pushed the waistband of his sweats down over his hips. I let them catch on his erection just to hear him gasp when it finally popped free. "Lie down on the bed."

He did, lying facedown, although I noticed how his hands shook. I put a condom on and added some lube. I climbed onto the bed, straddling his thighs the way he'd done to me that first time.

"Owen," he said, and I thought he might be near tears.

"Nick, listen to me. I know what I'm doing." I looked down at his gorgeous, round ass. I thought about what I was about to do. Did I know what I was doing? Not when it came to fucking him, no, I had no clue. But that wasn't the point. "I've read everything I can find on HIV transmission. Now, if you were about to fuck me, it would be a bit more of a risk, but that's not what either of us wants. It's less of a risk this way, and with the condom, it's negligible."

"Negligible, yes. But it's still there."

"You're right. But here's the thing, Nick: It's *my* risk. It's *my* decision. And I've decided it's worth it."

"Owen," he groaned. I could hear the conflict in his voice, desire warring with his conscience.

"Stop. I'm tired of this back-and-forth. You and I are happy together, aren't we?"

He sighed. "Yes."

"We have fun together. We're attracted to each other." I kissed his shoulder. "We love each other."

"Yes."

One word, but it made my heart soar. "Stop pretending like we have to be apart in order to protect me."

"I'm scared, Owen. I'm so scared of hurting you."

There was still lube on my fingers, and I pushed them between his firm cheeks, feeling for his opening. "Being pushed away hurts me more than this ever will."

He gave a soft sigh of surrender and slid his legs apart. Only an inch or so, since I was straddling him, but enough that I could trace his crack until I found what I sought. I caressed his rim, and his moan of pleasure was the most gratifying thing I'd ever heard.

"So what do you say?" I asked. "Want me to stop, or are you ready to admit that I'm right?"

The pillow muffled his throaty chuckle. "Right now I'll admit anything you want."

He pushed his ass toward my hand, and I slid my fingers into him. His body was so tight and warm, and all I could think about was how good it would feel around my cock.

I pulled my fingers out and tilted my erection toward him. It was awkward. I had to brace myself on my shortened left arm and hold my cock with my hand. I found his entrance, and he gasped when I pushed against him, but I knew the angle was all wrong.

"Nick," I started to say, but he was ahead of me. He reached back and helped me, guiding me into place. He pushed back and up with his hips. A bit of glorious pressure, and then I slid inside.

It took my breath away. I pushed in farther, trying to go slow, but the pleasure of it was so new, so intense, so overwhelming, I found it difficult to hold back. I indulged in a few thrusts to revel in how unbelievably good it felt. But then I reminded myself that this was supposed to be for him. Yes, it was my first time, and the urge to drive forward toward my own climax was strong, but I could do better by him than that.

I bit back my own moan and concentrated instead on Nick. I loved the sounds he made and the way he moved. I thrilled at the way his hips arched up to meet me. It took me a couple more thrusts to find my balance and my rhythm, rocking back and forth against his ass, sliding in and out of him, but once I did, it was perfect.

I leaned down to whisper into his ear. "Am I doing it right?"

"Yes! Dear God, yes. Please don't stop now."

"I don't intend to."

I sat up again.

And I fucked him.

It was glorious, better than I'd ever imagined. I felt strong and alive and magnificent. I felt victorious. I watched the muscles ripple across his back as he writhed and panted beneath me. I listened to his labored breath and his throaty moans. I stroked his flesh and squeezed his ass, and through it all, I rocked in and out of him, slow at first, but building, moving faster as our passion grew until our flesh was slapping together, until his hands holding the headboard were taut fists, his knuckles white. Until he was trembling, calling my name, begging me for more.

Until he came so hard he nearly screamed.

His body tightened around my cock. The strength of it surprised me, and I waited until the spasms had stopped to pull out of him. I hadn't come, but I didn't mind. This had been for him, and if I had my way, we'd have plenty of time later. I pulled off the condom—clumsily, but I didn't make too much of a mess—and tossed it in the trash. He lay beneath me, still shaking from the force of his orgasm, and I leaned down to kiss his shoulder.

"Owen," he whispered. He turned to take me in his arms. He rolled on top of me and buried his face in my neck. He was shaking, and his cheeks were damp. "I still worry this is a bad idea."

"We've both done our time in the cage. I think it's time we break free."

"I want you to be safe."

"To hell with safe. I'll take happy over safe any day of the week." I kissed his cheek. "You make me happy."

He laughed, a sad, choking sound. "You make me happy too."

"You're not acting very happy right now."

"I'm just not sure it's right. Not after what I did."

"You've wallowed in the guilt long enough. Yes, you made a mistake. But that doesn't mean you have to punish yourself for the rest of your life. You deserve to be loved. And to be happy." I kissed his forehead. "We both do."

He wasn't ready to stop fighting—not quite yet— but I knew we were close. I could feel it in the way he relaxed against me. In the way the tension left his shoulders. In the way the grief started to leave his voice. "Maybe you're right. Maybe I have been trying to punish myself."

"For getting sick to begin with?"

"Yes. And no. For what it did to my family more than anything. A few months after moving to Tucker Springs, I finally broke down and looked at June's pictures of that trip to Cancun, and I couldn't believe how much my mom had changed. It'd only been sixteen months, but it was like she'd aged ten years in that time. And it was all because of me."

"But do you really think she'd want you to pay for it by being miserable for the rest of your life?"

He laughed. "No. In fact she told me after she met you that she was glad I'd found somebody to love." He tightened his arms around me. "I do love you, more than you'll ever know."

"Then stop pulling away. Stop telling me we can't be together."

"What if you get sick?"

I almost laughed. Almost. "What if I slip in the tub tomorrow and break my neck? What if I walk out the door and get hit by a bus? What if I get struck by lightning?"

"None of those things will happen."

"Do you know that for a fact?"

He was silent for a moment, but he finally said, "I suppose not."

"I keep thinking, if I knew I was going to die tomorrow or next week or next month, would I say, 'Gee, good thing Nick and I played it safe'? No. I'd wish that we'd spent every single minute together. To hell with being safe."

"But Owen—"

"I'm not saying we be careless. I'm just saying, there are a lot of things that could go wrong, most of them completely out of our control. So why not embrace the things that are going right? I've spent my life feeling like a victim, but not anymore. And it's time for you to do the same thing. Stop letting yourself be a victim of the virus."

"Is it really that simple?"

"I think it is. Unlike my arm and your illness, this is a choice, Nick. It's a chance at happiness. A chance at joy. And I won't let it slip by. I won't go back to my cage. Not ever. I'd rather risk everything than live like that again."

He laid his head on my chest again and stroked my side. "I'm tired of the cage too."

"Then leave it behind." I grabbed a handful of his hair and pulled, forcing him to face me. "This really is our decision to make, Nick, and I choose this. I choose you."

He smiled, a slow, teasing smile that filled me with happiness. "Then I guess I have to choose you too."

I laughed at the joy of it—of finally seeing the real Nick again and of knowing the fight was over. I wrapped my arms around his neck. "Jesus. It's about damn time."

He chuckled and kissed my neck. My jaw. My cheek. "Pushing you away never worked anyway. For all of my noble intentions, I have no willpower at all when it comes to you."

"Thank goodness for that, or we never would have made it this far."

He laughed and reached down to caress my waning erection back to life. "Now that we have that settled," he said, "I'm ready for round two."

"Already?"

"You didn't come before."

The frankness of the statement made me blush a bit. "No, but I didn't want to be pushy."

"Why stop now?"

I laughed. "Should I apologize?"

"No." He kissed my neck. "The way I see it, we have eleven condoms left and five years of abstinence to make up for."

"Sounds like I'm in for a long day. You may have to make me breakfast first."

"Fair enough." He kissed me again. "Owen?"

"Yes."

"You really are my hero."

And you're mine.

Epilogue

February

"COME ON," Nick urged. "Let me see it!"

I'd finally taken Seth up on his offer for a discount on my first tattoo. My upper arm still burned from the bite of the needle. I put my hand over the bandage. "He said to keep it covered for five hours."

"We'll cover it back up. Just let me peek."

"You'll laugh at me."

"So what's your plan? You're going to somehow keep your arm hidden from me forever?"

He was right, of course. I was being ridiculous. But what had seemed like a good idea when I'd gone into Ink Springs suddenly made me feel silly. Too late to turn back, though. It was now a permanent part of me.

I sighed and presented my arm for his inspection. Nick gently peeled off the tape and lifted the bit of gauze.

I was right. He did laugh. But it wasn't mockery. He laughed at the intimacy of a shared joke as he looked at it: the red-and-yellow Superman logo tattooed on my left biceps. He leaned over to kiss my shoulder. "It's perfect."

He was reapplying the tape when his doorbell rang. We still hadn't quite decided which apartment we were living in. Mine had more windows. His had the piano. For now, we occupied both.

"Are you expecting somebody?" he asked.

"Am I ever?"

"Maybe Nathan?"

"No." Nathan and I had become good friends over the past couple of months, but I knew he wouldn't stop by unannounced. I opened the door and found myself facing my past: Regina.

"Hi, Erwin," she said, obviously confused. "I thought you lived upstairs."

"It's Owen. And I do." *Mostly.*

"Oh. Well, can I talk to whoever lives down here?"

Nick came up behind me, practically radiating Annoyed Boyfriend. I didn't miss the admiring look she gave him or the way she dismissed me to smile at him.

"Can I help you?" he asked.

"It's about the piano," she said. "I miss it. I was wondering if there was any chance of me getting it back? I could even buy it from you, if you're not asking too much, and I'd be happy to pay for a moving company."

My piano, I thought. *And my boyfriend.* It was with great deal of satisfaction that I pushed Nick back inside and said to her, as I closed the door, "I'm afraid it's not for sale."

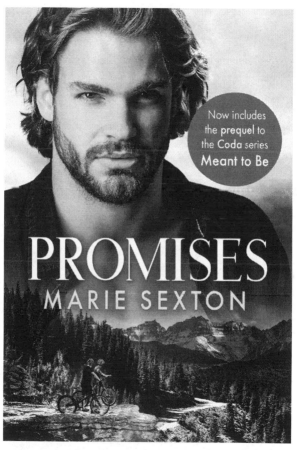

Can a man who loves his small hometown trust it to love him back?

Jared Thomas has lived in the mountain town of Coda, Colorado, his whole life. He can't imagine living anywhere else. But Jared's opportunities are limited—the only other gay man in town is twice his age, and although Jared originally planned to be a teacher, the backlash that might accompany the gig keeps him working at his family's store instead.

Then Matt Richards moves to town.

Matt may not be into guys, but he doesn't care that Jared is. A summer camping and mountain biking together cements their friendship, but when Matt realizes he's attracted to Jared, he panics and withdraws, leaving Jared all too aware of what he's missing.

Facing Matt's affair with a local woman, his disapproving family, and harassment from Matt's coworkers, Jared fears they'll never find a way to be together. But for the first time, he has the courage to try… if he can only convince Matt.

Meant to Be

Jared has simple goals for his freshman year of college: make friends, lose his virginity, come out, and maybe fall in love. He doesn't anticipate getting caught between his friend Bryan and Bryan's flamboyant ex. Through the awkwardness, Jared learns love doesn't always mean sex and the most meaningful connections might have nothing to do with romance.

Chapter 1

THE WHOLE thing started because of Lizzy's Jeep. If it hadn't been for that, I might not have met Matt. And maybe he wouldn't have felt the need to prove himself. And maybe nobody would have been hurt.

But I'm getting ahead of myself. Like I said, it started with Lizzy's Jeep. Lizzy is the wife of my brother Brian, and they were expecting their first child in the fall. She decided her old Wrangler, which she'd had since college, wasn't going to cut it as a family vehicle. So she parked it out front of our shop with a handwritten For Sale sign in the window.

"The shop" had come to us via my grandfather. Originally, it'd been a hardware store. At some point, auto parts had been added as well. When my grandpa died, my dad took over the store, and when he died, it passed to Brian, Lizzy, and me. Normally, I didn't mind tending the place, but it was a gorgeous spring day in

Colorado, and at that moment, I would have rather been outside, enjoying the sunshine. Instead, I was sitting with my feet on the counter, dreaming of what might have been.

That's when he came in.

He caught my attention right away, simply because he wasn't from around here. I've lived in Coda my whole life, not counting the five years I spent in Fort Collins, at the university, and I knew everybody in town, by sight if not by name. So he was either visiting somebody in the area or just passing through. We're not a tourist town, but people do bump into us occasionally, either looking for four-wheel drive trails or on their way to one of the dude ranches farther up the road.

He certainly didn't look like one of the middle-aged suckers who frequented the dude ranches. He was probably in his early thirties, taller than me by several inches, putting him just over six feet tall, with military-short black hair and a couple of days' worth of dark stubble on his cheeks. He wore jeans, a plain black T-shirt, and cowboy boots. Broad shoulders and big arms showed he worked out.

In short, he was drop-dead gorgeous.

"That Jeep run?" His voice was deep with a little bit of a drawl. Not Deep South drawl, but the vowels were definitely longer than a Coloradan.

"You bet. Runs great."

"Hmmm." He glanced out the window at it. "Why're you selling it?"

"Not me. My sister-in-law. She says it'll be too hard to get a car seat in the back. She bought a Cherokee instead."

He looked a little confused by that, which told me he didn't have kids himself. "So it drives okay?"

"Perfect. Want to try it out? I've got the keys right here."

His eyebrows went up. "You need collateral or something? I can leave my license."

I think at that point, he could've talked me into anything. My knees wobbled a bit. Was there really a touch of green in those steel-gray eyes? I hoped I sounded casual when I said, "I'll go with you. I know the roads around here. We can take it up one of the easy trails so you can see how it handles."

"What about the store? Hate to leave you short-handed during rush hour." He raised an eyebrow toward the empty store, one corner of his mouth barely twitching up. "Won't your boss be mad if you leave?"

I laughed. "I'm one of the owners, so I can slack off if I want to." I turned and called into the back room, "Hey, Ringo?"

Our one employee came warily out of the back. He was always skittish with me, and if Lizzy wasn't around, he made a point of keeping his distance. I think he expected me to make a pass at him. He was seventeen with stringy black hair and bad skin. He probably weighed a buck five soaking wet. I didn't have the heart to tell him he wasn't my type.

"Yeah?"

"Hold the fort. I'll be back in an hour or so." I turned back to my tall, dark stranger. "Let's go."

Once we were in the Jeep, he held his hand out to me. "I'm Matt Richards."

"Jared Thomas." His grip was strong, but he wasn't one of those guys who had to break your hand to prove how macho he is.

"Which way?"

"Turn left. We'll just drive up to the Rock."

"What's that?"

"What it sounds like—a big fucking rock. It's nothing spectacular. People go up there to picnic. And the teenagers go there to park or to get high."

He frowned a little at that. I was starting to think he didn't smile much. I, on the other hand, was grinning ear to ear. Getting out of the store for a few minutes, especially to head into the mountains, was enough to brighten my day considerably. Doing it in the company of the best-looking guy I'd seen in a hell of a long time? Yeah. It was already the best day I'd had in ages.

"So what brings you to our fine metropolis?" I asked him.

"I just moved here."

"Really? Why in the world would you want to do that?"

"Why not?" His tone was bantering, although his face was still serious. "You live here, don't you? Is it that bad?"

"Well, no. I love it here. That's why I've never left. But, you know, the town is dying. More people moving out than moving in. Towns along the Front Range are booming, but nobody wants to live up here and commute."

"I was just hired by the Coda PD."

"You're a cop?"

He raised an eyebrow at me with obvious amusement. "Is that a problem?"

"Well, no, but I wish I hadn't told you about the kids coming up here to get high."

"Don't worry. I won't tell them you're the rat." So, the good officer wasn't completely without humor. "You've lived here your whole life?" He didn't sound curious so much as like he was just trying to make casual conversation.

"Yep. Except for the years I spent in college."

"And you own the store?"

"Me and my brother and his wife. It's not a big moneymaker or anything, but we manage. Brian's an accountant, and he has other clients, so he mostly just does the books. Lizzy and I run the shop."

"But you went to college?" Now he sounded genuinely curious.

"Yeah, I went to Colorado State. I have degrees in physics and elementary education. I have my teacher's certificate too, for all the good it's doing me."

"Why aren't you a teacher?"

"I didn't want to let Brian and Lizzy down." That wasn't entirely true, but I didn't want to tell him the real reason: that I didn't want to deal with the fallout of being a gay high school teacher in a small town. "There isn't anyone else to cover the shop. We can't afford a full-time employee. Well, we could if they didn't want benefits, but they do. So instead, we just have Ringo, part-time. We get half his salary back, 'cause he spends his paychecks on stuff for his car, so it works out okay." I laughed. "Ringo. That can't be his real name." Good lord, I was babbling like an idiot. "Sorry I'm talking so much. I'm sure I'm boring you."

He looked right at me and said, "Not at all."

We reached the parking area at the end of the road. "You'll have to turn around here."

He stopped the Jeep and glanced around. There were no other cars. "I don't see any rock."

"Just up the trail a bit. Want to walk up there?"

His face brightened a little. "You bet."

So we walked down the trail, through Ponderosa pines and Douglas firs and aspens that were just starting to bud, to one of the rocky abutments that must have helped give the Rockies their name. The Colorado mountains are full of these giant piles of boulders, rounded by wind and time, covered with dry sage—and rust-colored lichen. This one was about twenty feet high on the downhill side. If you walked up the hill, you could practically walk right out onto it. But what's the fun in that? These rocks just beg to be climbed.

Once we reached the top, we sat down. The view wasn't really any different from there. We could see down the trail to the Jeep, but other than that, it was just more trees, more rocks, more mountains. I love Colorado, but this type of view can be found in hundreds of spots. I was surprised to hear a contented sigh from Matt. When I looked at him, his face showed amazement.

"Man, I love Colorado. I'm from Oklahoma. This is better, believe me."

He turned to look at me, squinting into the sun, and I almost quit breathing. His skin was tan, and his eyes were shining. Yeah. Definitely a hint of green in them. "Thanks for bringing me up here."

"Anytime." And I meant it.

Chapter 2

MATT CAME by the shop the next day, cash in hand, to buy the Jeep. It was a Saturday, normally one of our busier days, so Lizzy and I were both working.

"Will you join me for a beer?" Matt asked. He'd shaved that morning, and it made him look several years younger. Man, he was cute.

"I'd love to, but you'll have to give me a rain check. I'm having dinner with the family."

"Oh." He sounded disappointed. "Well, maybe another time...."

"Wait a minute," Lizzy interrupted, grinning ear to ear. I could tell by the look on her face she thought she was doing me a huge favor. "Why don't you join us? We're just having dinner up at the house. We'd love to have you."

I probably should have seen that coming. Still, it surprised me when Matt agreed.

Once he was gone, I tried not to look at Lizzy, who was practically bouncing on her toes, wearing the goofiest smile I'd seen in a long time. She has blonde hair that seems to fly all over the place when she moves, and blue eyes, which at the moment were shining with excitement. I suppose she falls somewhere between "lovely" and "cute as a button," and I swear she could charm the stars down out of the sky if she tried.

"Well?" she finally asked.

"Well, what?" I knew I was blushing and hated myself for it.

"You know what." She smacked me on the arm. "He's hot! And he asked you out. Aren't you excited?" The fact was, I didn't have many friends. Most of my buddies from high school were married with kids. The ones who weren't married were all troublemakers who spent their nights drinking at the bar. Lizzy was probably the best friend I had in the world, and I knew she hoped I'd find somebody.

"I don't think he meant it as a date."

Her smile faltered a little. "You don't?"

"Does he look gay to you?"

"Well, no. But neither do you, so that obviously doesn't mean anything, and you know it. He wanted to take you out and was disappointed that he wasn't going to have you to himself. I think he's interested." The smile came back in its full glory.

I knew better than to get my hopes up. Needless to say, I never planned to be in my thirties and still alone, but being gay in a town this small isn't easy. Colorado isn't exactly a gay mecca; it's not the Bible Belt, but it's not San Francisco either. Most of the town knows about me, and most of them even accept me, but a few still look the other way when I pass them in the grocery store or refuse to deal with me when they come into the shop.

People always ask me when I knew I was gay. I guess they think I had some epiphany—lights flashing and horns blaring—but it wasn't like that for me. It was more of a culmination of events.

I suppose the first clues came early in puberty as I compared myself to my brother, Brian, two years my elder. While he was hanging up posters of Cindy Crawford and Samantha Fox, I was putting up only cars and the Denver Broncos. I knew he found girls enticing and fascinating in a way I didn't understand, but I didn't worry about it much.

One weekend when I was fifteen, my dad went to a Broncos game and bought me a poster showing the whole team with the cheerleaders arrayed around them in various provocative poses. Brian helped me hang it up, and then we stepped back to admire it.

"Which one do you think is the best-looking?" Brian asked me.

"Steve Atwater," I said without even thinking about it.

He laughed, but it was a nervous kind of laugh, like he wasn't sure if I was pulling his leg or not. When I glanced his way, I found him staring at me with a look on his face that would eventually become very familiar: part humor, part confusion, part concern. I was embarrassed. I knew my answer was wrong, and yet, I wasn't really sure why.

"No," he said, "I meant which one of the *cheerleaders*?"

In truth, I'd barely noticed them.

Soon my friends were swapping skin magazines with shaking hands and boastful laughs. I wasn't exactly sure what they felt when they looked at them, but it was pretty clear it wasn't the same as the mild embarrassment they elicited in me.

It wasn't until I met Tom that I realized exactly how different I was. Tom played football with Brian. They were best friends. I was sixteen; they were eighteen. From the moment he walked through our front door, I was infatuated with him. I could barely speak to him but couldn't keep my eyes off him. His laugh was enough to elicit physical responses that caused me to always have a schoolbook in my hand when he was in the house—not because I was such a good student, but because I needed to be able to cover myself quickly. I walked a fine line between wanting to see him as much as possible and wanting to stay out of his sight. I caught Brian watching me again with the same looks he had given me the day I blurted out Steve Atwater's name: concern, bemusement, embarrassment. It was something of a relief when the two of them finally graduated and went off to college.

After that, I was pretty sure, although I never said anything to anybody. I faked my way through high school. I never tried out for football because I was afraid of the complications that could arise in the locker room, if only in my imagination. I had a few dates with girls, but they were mostly group dates; we held hands a few times, and a couple of them even kissed me. The kisses were, for me at least, completely uninspiring, bordering on disturbing, and it never went further than that.

Once I made it to college, away from home, I finally allowed myself to experiment. I met guys at the club or at the gym and had a few brief but meaningless affairs. Never found anything I would have called love, but I knew after that, without a doubt, that I was gay. Maybe I should have moved somewhere else after graduating, but no place else would have felt like home. Still, hot new cop or not, chances of finding a partner in Coda were almost nonexistent, and chances of me ending up alone seemed depressingly high.

Marie Sexton is the author of over thirty published works. She's written contemporary romance, science fiction, fantasy, dystopian fiction, historical short stories, and a few odd genre mash-ups. The one thing they all have in common? They all feature men falling in love with other men. Her first novel, *Promises*, was published in January 2010 and is considered a classic in the gay romance genre.

Marie is the recipient of multiple Rainbow Awards, as well as the CRW Award of Excellence in 2012. She was also a finalist for a Lambda Literary Award in 2017. Her books have been translated into seven languages.

Marie lives in Colorado. She's a fan of just about anything that involves muscular young men piling on top of each other. In particular, she loves the Denver Broncos and enjoys going to the games with her husband. Her imaginary friends often tag along. Marie has one daughter, two cats, and one dog, all of whom seem bent on destroying what remains of her sanity. She loves them anyway.

You can find her at mariesexton.net, and on Facebook, Instagram, and Twitter.

Instagram: www.instagram.com/mariesexton.author

Facebook: www.facebook.com/MarieSexton.author

Twitter: @MarieSexton

WHERE
NERVES END

A TUCKER SPRINGS NOVEL

L.A. WITT

A Tucker Springs Novel

Welcome to Tucker Springs, Colorado, where you'll enjoy beautiful mountain views and the opportunity to study at one of two prestigious universities—if you can afford to live there.

Jason Davis is in pain. Still smarting from a bad breakup, he struggles to pay both halves of an overwhelming mortgage and balance the books at his floundering business. As if the emotional and financial pain weren't enough, the agony of a years-old shoulder injury keeps him up at night. When he faces a choice between medication and insomnia, he takes a friend's advice and gives acupuncture a try.

Acupuncturist Michael Whitman is a single dad striving to make ends meet, and his landlord just hiked the rent. When new patient Jason, a referral from a mutual friend, suggests a roommate arrangement could benefit them both, Michael seizes the opportunity.

Getting a roommate might be the best idea Jason's ever had—if it weren't for his attraction to Michael, who seems to be allergic to wearing shirts in the house. Still, a little unresolved sexual tension is a small price to pay for pain and financial relief. He'll keep his hands and feelings to himself since Michael is straight… isn't he?

www.dreamspinnerpress.com

SECOND HAND

A TUCKER SPRINGS NOVEL

MARIE SEXTON
HEIDI CULLINAN

A Tucker Springs Novel

Paul Hannon flunked out of vet school. His fiancée left him. He can barely afford his rent, and he hates his house. About the only things he has left are a pantry full of his ex's kitchen gadgets and a lot of emotional baggage. He could really use a win—and that's when he meets El.

Pawnbroker El Rozal is a cynic. His own family's dysfunction has taught him that love and relationships lead to misery. Despite that belief, he keeps making up excuses to see Paul again. Paul, who doesn't seem to realize that he's talented and kind and worthy. Paul, who's not over his ex-fiancée and is probably straight anyway. Paul, who's so blind to El's growing attraction, even asking him out on dates doesn't seem to tip him off.

El may not do relationships, but something has to give. If he wants to keep Paul, he'll have to convince him he's worthy of love—and he'll have to admit that attachment might not be so bad after all.

www.dreamspinnerpress.com

DIRTY
LAUNDRY

A TUCKER SPRINGS NOVEL

HEIDI CULLINAN

A Tucker Springs Novel

Sometimes you have to get dirty to come clean.

When muscle-bound Denver Rogers effortlessly dispatches the frat boys harassing grad student Adam Ellery at the Tucker Springs laundromat, Adam's thank-you turns into impromptu sex over the laundry table. The problem comes when they exchange numbers. What if Adam wants to meet again and discovers Denver is a high-school dropout with a learning disability who works as a bouncer at a local gay bar? Or what if Denver calls Adam only to learn while he might be brilliant in the lab, outside of it he has crippling social anxiety and obsessive-compulsive disorder?

Either way, neither of them can shake the memory of their laundromat encounter. Despite their fears of what the other might think, they can only remember how good the other one feels. The more they get together, the kinkier things become. They're both a little bent, but in just the right ways.

Maybe the secret to staying together isn't to keep things clean and proper. Maybe it's best to keep their laundry just a little bit dirty.

www.dreamspinnerpress.com

TATTOOS

COVET THY NEIGHBOR

A TUCKER SPRINGS NOVEL

L.A. WITT

A Tucker Springs Novel

Welcome to Tucker Springs, Colorado, where sparks fly when opposites attract—but are some obstacles too great to overcome?

When tattoo artist Seth Wheeler meets his new neighbor, it's like a revelation. Darren Romero is everything Seth wants in a man: hot, clever, single, and interested. For a minute he seems perfect. Then Darren drops the bomb: he moved to Tucker Springs to be a pastor at the New Light Church.

As a gay man whose parents threw him out, Seth has a strict policy of keeping believers at arm's length for self-preservation. But Darren's perseverance and the chemistry bubbling between them steadily wear down his defenses.

In a small town like Tucker Springs, Seth can't avoid Darren—or how much he wants him. Which means he needs to decide what's more important: protecting himself, or his feelings for his neighbor.

www.dreamspinnerpress.com